THE POWE

The Power to Forgive and Other Stories

Avinuo Kire

zubaan

ZUBAAN
an imprint of Kali for Women
128B Shahpur Jat, 1st floor
NEW DELHI 110 049
Email: contact@zubaanbooks.com
Website: www.zubaanbooks.com

This edition published by Zubaan Publishers Pvt. Ltd., 2015

Copyright © Avinuo Kire 2015

All rights reserved

10 9 8 7 6 5 4 3 2 1

ISBN 978 93 83074 92 1

Zubaan is an independent feminist publishing house based in New Delhi with a strong academic and general list. It was set up as an imprint of India's first feminist publishing house, Kali for Women, and carries forward Kali's tradition of publishing world quality books to high editorial and production standards. *Zubaan* means tongue, voice, language, speech in Hindustani. Zubaan is a non-profit publisher, working in the areas of the humanities, social sciences, as well as in fiction, general non-fiction, and books for children and young adults under its Young Zubaan imprint.

Typeset by Jojy Philip, New Delhi 110 015
Printed at Raj Press, R-3 Inderpuri, New Delhi 110 012

For my parents
and for Atsa

Contents

The Power To Forgive

She sat on bended knees, rifling through pages of old documents and other papers, some which would remain forever necessary and some which had long fulfilled their purpose. She had never been a particularly organised person. Marksheets, old Christmas and birthday cards, and various outdated church programmes were all jammed inside a single brown cardboard file with the words 'Government of Nagaland' on the cover. A page of paper made a ruffling sound of protest as she crumpled it into a ball and threw it towards the waste bin.

She was getting married soon. Sorting out her meagre belongings was the first phase of preparation for the new life she would soon embark upon. He had proposed a few nights ago and she had shyly accepted, like they both knew she would. She was twenty-eight and still retained youth's fresh-faced sweetness. He, on the other hand, was an unattractive man already well into his mid-forties; but she had no complaints. If anything, she was grateful that he had asked her at all. She had long resigned herself to the likelihood that marital life was not to be part of her destiny. Therefore, it did not matter to her that he was unemployed or that he could seldom hold his liquor. He had asked her to be his and that excused all his weaknesses. A feeling of affection overcame her as she recalled his uncharacteristic solemnity while discussing plans for their impending nuptials. 'I shall ask my elder brother and grand aunt to ask for your hand in marriage. You can tell your parents to expect a visit from my relatives this Saturday,' he had promised. To be treated so sensitively, as if she was as pure and untouched as any other sheltered young woman, touched her, endeared him to her. Sometimes she would be suspicious when other men treated her likewise. 'Don't you know?' she would want to question them.

Shaking free from her habit of ruminating endlessly, she gathered the papers together and tapped them against the floor to align them. Upon that innocent act, a modest-sized newspaper clipping suddenly slipped from within the collective pile and fell to the floor. 'FATHER FORGIVES MAN WHO RAPED DAUGHTER,' read the headline in bold capital letters. 'In a supreme act of Christian forgiveness...' But she did not have to read, did not need to. She had felt the weight of the words even before they hit the smooth mud floor. She had been acutely aware of this clipping while sorting out her papers, and had been very careful to ignore it. Yet there it was, forcing her to confront once again a single devastating memory that clung to her entire past like an overpowering rotten smell, effectively erasing all other remembrances. It seemed to her that memory was partial to pain and loss. A torrent of emotions: the old familiar wave of anger, shame and betrayal, a mind-numbing tornado of

resentment that always left her with disastrous headaches–
all these threatened to crush her happy mood.

She picked up the tattered newspaper clipping with
distaste and tucked it beneath the mattress. She knew that
she no longer wanted to preserve it in her file. At the same
time, she could not bring herself to destroy it. A thought
struck her as she resisted her immediate impulse to add the
paper to the nearby trash. Perhaps it was quite natural for a
person to form attachments to anything. One simply had to
live with something long enough.

It happened sixteen years ago, when she was only twelve.
Her rapist had been her paternal uncle. To this day, though
other details had become vague with the passing of time, she
still distinctly remembered the nauseating smell of him – a
mixture of sweat together with a faint eggy sourness – and
the hot wave of heavy panting. She was alone in the house
and her uncle had left hurriedly after committing the heinous
deed. He had murmured something to her before leaving but
she could not remember what it was. A curious and kindly
neighbour had forced her way into their neat three-roomed
bamboo house and found her curled up in a corner, dazed
and crying. Upon the woman's concerned questioning, she
had related what happened.

The little Naga village rose up in righteous outrage when
the incident came to light. The story was reported in the local
newspapers and various organisations voiced their fervent
condemnation of the incident. Never had her little village
received so much attention. She remembered her mother
comforting her in the hospital while some police personnel
wrote down her statements. She also remembered a group
of women from some women's rights organisation who

came to visit her all the way from Kohima, the capital town. Her mother had made such a fuss over the women, and had related the horrific incident in detail, as though she had been a silent witness. This all happened a long time ago. She had known life before and after the unfolding of these events. It frustrated her, therefore, how those few weeks often seemed to sum up the story of her existence.

Over the years, if not reconciled to it, she had learned to accept what had happened to her. There were moments she even forgot; happy times while gathering water, or washing clothes beside the village river with other girls, when she imagined she was as carefree as any one of them. But such light-heartedness was always short-lived. 'People will think you have no shame!' Her mother was always quick to remind her. Mother never failed to lament the stigma that had become attached to their family because of her and, at the same time, never encouraged anyone, her least of all, to revisit the incident. Mother had become a scared woman, always careful to maintain an emotionally detached relationship with her own daughter, fearful that intimacy would allow for indulgent exchanges. Though nothing was ever said, she sometimes felt that her mother blamed her for what had happened. She sensed judgement through her mother's furtive glances, her thinly pursed lips, her grimaces. She thought no one understood the meaning of silences more than her mother; in time she too had learned the language well. She would repeatedly agonise over the events that had unfolded that fateful day; over whether she ought to have been more alert, more wary, fought harder. But above all, her most agonising thought was whether life would have been simpler if she had kept that one day of her life a secret. She often wondered whether things would have been different had her mother discovered her first. Somehow, she knew she could get over the violation of her body; she could bear her shame in private. It only became intolerable when society "shared" the shame.

She had been belatedly informed of her father's decision to forgive her uncle. A few weeks after the uproar had died down, her father came to her room and sat down at the edge of her bed. He said so many things about forgiveness, justice and family honour. He said so much in such a grave voice. But nothing had prepared her for what he announced in the end. He stood up slowly as he spoke, indicating to her that his speech was nearing its end. With an air of parental authority, he said:

'I have decided to forgive your uncle. But you need never worry about him; you will never see or hear from that man again.'

The taut stirrings of a strange and alien emotion bubbled deep within her at the words; feelings much too complicated for a child of twelve. Frustrated at not being able to express what she felt, she burst into helpless tears. Her father, a good but undemonstrative man, looked at her uneasily and said in a heavy voice, 'One day you will realise that this is the right thing to do. Hatred will only destroy us.' He said something about her uncle being in jail and also being excommunicated from their village. But nothing mattered more than her angry resentment towards her own father. She did not realise then that the alien emotion she felt was betrayal. 'As if *he* had been the victim,' she would wondrously voice aloud to herself many times in the years to come. That night, she had an especially vivid nightmare. In her dream, her uncle's giant face seemed pressed to her and she could not escape. She tried to scream, but her voice died as the face of the enemy slowly morphed into her beloved father's worn features.

Sixteen years had passed since. Once a gay and cheerful child, she had now become withdrawn and reserved. She was still a dutiful daughter to her parents but it ended there. Her relationships with other people could be described as cordial at best. Though always polite, she was unable to forge close friendships. She had heard that her rapist uncle was now a free man. He had served seven years behind bars. Seven years in exchange for devastating her life. He had actually gone on to marry, have children and was now living with his family in Dimapur district. She bitterly wondered who had married him. She often broke out in a cold sweat whenever she came across anyone who resembled her uncle. Her biggest fear was the thought of meeting her uncle now, after all these years. This constant anxiety resulted in recurring nightmares. She knew it was unreasonable but she actually felt ashamed, even of him. As if she had played a role in her own disgrace.

Except for the youngest, all her other siblings– three sisters and two brothers – had married and relocated elsewhere. She was not particularly close to any of them. The one person in the world she truly held dear was her youngest brother Pele. He was the only one who saw her as she was; without sympathy or judgement, without the shadow of what had happened to her hanging over her head. As incredible as it seemed to her, her sixteen-year-old brother actually looked up to her as an elder sister and she loved him all the more for it. And now, she was finally getting married and soon to move out of the house she thought she was destined to live her remaining life and die in. A wry smile touched her face as she realised that she was like all women after all. Shifting required a sizeable amount of baggage, although in her case, the bulk of it remained unseen. It had become a part of her; she could not leave it behind.

'Your father will need a new suit,' her mother remarked. She looked at her mother, contentedly picking stones out of the rice while helping her make plans for the wedding. It had been a long time since she had seen her mother so serene. She realised with sadness that she was not the only one who had changed. Her mother, once a warm and somewhat boisterous woman, had developed a quaint meekness, a pessimistic attitude so unlike that of the fearless woman she had once been. Her mother, she decided, had developed three different personalities: fierce towards her husband, long-suffering towards her children, and timid towards society in general. A long time ago, she had witnessed her parents quarrelling after a visit to her paternal grandmother. Eavesdropping through bamboo walls, she gathered that Grandmother had blamed her mother for what had happened to her.

'You stood there without defending me while your mother accused me of being a bad mother! How dare she blame me for our daughter's...!' Her mother's angry tirade ended in sobs without her completing the sentence. Her father had replied, 'You are overreacting! She does not blame you, how could she? All she said was that mothers should be careful not to leave young daughters unattended!' Her younger self did not wish to listen anymore. She put little hands over her ears and faked sleep until it finally came.

Mother poured the cleaned rice inside an empty barrel,

humming a soft lullaby while doing so. Her mother did not gossip. Perhaps she used to, but not anymore. She had too much at stake. 'We each have our cross to bear,' was her mother's ambiguous response to everything and anything unsavoury about anyone. She sometimes pitied her mother's naivety in hoping that by not judging others, she would escape being judged herself.

Her silent reverie was broken by her mother's quizzical glance.

'Girl! Where is your mind, did you hear what I just said? Your father will need a proper suit to walk you down the aisle.'

She braced herself; she had been prepared for this issue.

'Yes of course. Actually, I am planning to ask Pele to walk me down the aisle,' she replied tentatively.

'Nonsense! Your father should have that honour.'

'No, I want Pele to give me away, it's my wedding after all,' she said firmly.

Her mother gave her a pained look but did not argue. She simply said, 'Think about it, your father will be very hurt.'

She felt a savage satisfaction at Mother's words.

Her brother's reaction was predictable. 'Dear sister! Of course I shall be honoured, but don't you think it should be father?'

'I'd rather you do it,' she said stubbornly

'It's your wedding,' he agreed.

She did not feel the same satisfaction.

Traditional wisdom discouraged long engagements, predicting that they gave rise to second thoughts and gossip. And so, a date was fixed quickly and it wasn't long before the wedding preparations began. The villagers arrived in droves to help; different groups for different work. The menfolk came together to construct a makeshift bamboo pavilion for the reception, and later helped to butcher two cows and a pig for the wedding feast. The women arrived to decorate the reception area and helped with the cooking and cleaning. The villagers felt good about being kind and generous to her; she was their tragic child. As for the bride-to-be, for all her cynicism, she experienced a renewed faith in human goodness. She found it overwhelming that all the fuss and hectic preparations were for her benefit. Also, her once antagonistic relationship with her mother had silently begun to heal of its own accord; the two women had never been as close as they were now. The stress and underlying tension of their relationship had slowly begun to disappear ever since the night of her engagement. It was as if her becoming a bride had finally released her mother from her unhappiness.

The brief period of engagement was the happiest time in her life; so much so that she felt a sense of loss as the wedding date drew closer. The only thing that marred her happiness was the niggling uneasiness that persisted whenever she thought of her father. He had calmly accepted that her brother would be walking her down the aisle but she knew he was disappointed. She was still his daughter, after all.

She knew that he was a good father and in other circumstances, she would have adored him. However aloof, he was an honest, hard-working man and provided for his family the best way he could. An invisible barrier between father and daughter had been erected the night her father informed her of his decision. It was the last that they ever discussed what had happened. She had been angry and resolutely avoided speaking to him the first few months, and he had let her be. In time, as she entered adolescence, she became too ashamed to ever broach the painful topic. In vain, she waited for him to take the initiative. Knowing her father's reclusive nature now, she knew it had been folly to expect that of him. So then, words that should have been spoken were bottled up instead, and it daily watered the seed of resentment sown deep within. In her subconscious mind, her decision to deny her father his right to give her away was her manner of punishing him for denying her the right to forgive a crime committed against her. Then again, seeing his calm acceptance of her decision, she wondered whether he was all that affected by it. Had she managed to hurt him as deeply as he had her? It tormented her, this unfinished business. Finally, she resolved that she would tell him how she felt, how he had let her down. She decided to tell him everything, all her pent-up feelings. Only then would she find the peace that constantly eluded her.

She found an opportune time the evening before her wedding. She had been sent home early to get sufficient rest and sleep for her big day tomorrow. Her mother, brother and the rest of her married siblings who had arrived for the wedding with their families were still at the reception venue, making some final arrangements. She knew her father was alone at home. She carefully rehearsed her speech, the precise words to say and how to begin. Soon, she found herself approaching the house. Her rapidly beating heart compelled her to linger outside the front door for a while. She took a deep breath in order to steady her frazzled nerves. As she did so, a raw guttural sound from inside the house startled her. She quietly pushed open the door and stepped inside. Then she heard some inaudible words broken by fervent sobs. The sound came from inside her parents' bedroom. With her heart hammering against her chest, she looked inside the room, and what she saw made her freeze. Her weeping father sat awkwardly on a chair, elbows on his knees and hands supporting his bent head, revealing a mass of prematurely greying hair. Laid beside him on the bed was his new suit for her wedding and a rumpled copy of the church solemnisation programme. She had never in her life seen her father show any strong emotion, let alone cry. It embarrassed and distressed her at the same time. She was not sure what to do.

Her father was unaware of her presence, and so she silently stepped back and retreated to her room. Feeling numb, she sat on her bed and tried to collect herself. She looked around the bare room, stripped of all belongings but for three pieces of luggage neatly stacked beside her bed. All worldly evidence of her twenty-eight years packed inside three pieces of luggage; a worn-out VIP suitcase which had once belonged to her father and two colourful bags. One she had owned for some time, and the other was a wedding gift from her parents. She made a mental checklist of the things she wanted to take to her new life. Her soon-to-be husband had revealed a surprisingly kind and thoughtful nature during their time together. Despite his shortcomings, she knew that he could make her happy if she allowed him to. Her thoughts turned towards the tragic figure a couple of rooms away. Instinct told her that she was the cause of his profound grief. She closed her eyes and her body trembled. She knew then what she must do; for the first time, she wanted to do what she should have done. Her right hand reached under the mattress and pulled out the newspaper clipping, cosseted for too long. For the first time, she felt no dread of the words staring back at her. She had encouraged herself to play the victim too long. It was now time to let go. She walked towards the kitchen and threw the incriminating paper into the fireplace. She did not bother to look as the flames consumed it in mere seconds.

With every brisk, purposeful step she took, the carefully constructed wall around her heart seemed to lighten; each brick loosened and crumbled, one by one. With a confidence she had never felt before, she pushed open the final door. Her father looked up and on seeing her, stood clumsily. He faced her unashamed, a grown man with tears and snot streaking his cheeks. It did not matter who closed the distance; they embraced and he kissed her forehead. In that loving act, the world of words mattered no more.

Tomorrow would bring yet another day and with it, new challenges. But somehow she knew now that she would be all right. She even thought about the fear that dogged her; the idea of accidently running into her uncle. This possibility no longer filled her with dread. In fact, she hoped she did meet him. She would hold her head high and look him in the eye. He would know that he did not 'ruin' her, that his evil had not tainted her. She revelled in the liberating absence of the bitterness which had long plagued her weary soul. For the first time since forever, she finally felt free.

Solie

They removed him today; the old peon-cum-sweeper in my office. He had been tagged 'lazy' and 'inefficient' in performing his duties, which basically consisted of opening and locking the office premises, in addition to sweeping and scrubbing the entire building every morning. 'What to do! He has already been warned repeatedly!' they comforted themselves by saying. Old Mr. Vilelie justified their action in his deeply sonorous voice, 'Even the Bible has said, "If a man will not work, he shall not eat."'Everyone nodded in appreciation of what they considered to be a thoroughly sound argument. And so, that was the end of Mr. Solie Naga or 'Solie', as he was simply referred to by us all, young and old alike. He had been appointed under contract service and had served the department for exactly one year and half a month. His application for extension of contract had been consensually rejected.

It seemed to me that they need not have bothered feeling so guilty. In actuality, it felt like Solie didn't care much about his job and even less about the extension of his service. I knew this because I was the one who kept reminding him to submit an application in time before the expiry of his contract. He kept procrastinating, always mumbling some excuse or the other. I thought that perhaps he was too proud to ask for help, so I even offered to help him write his application. He put me well and truly in my place by refusing my offer and handing in a beautifully typed letter the following day. Never have I met anyone with so much pride as Solie. He was a tall and scrawny looking man, always in blue and white rubber chappals and a hand woven traditional Naga bag slung diagonally across his upper torso. What drew our attention the first time we set eyes on Solie was the way he held his broom. He gripped it like a rifle with the handle firmly against his chest and the other end resting upon his shoulder. 'There goes Solie with his bonduk!' we often joked amongst ourselves. If he heard us, he gave no indication of it. Perhaps he did not do so because it did not bother or affect him in the least.

He intrigued me, this aloof and elderly man. To be fair to my superiors, they had every reason to remove Solie. The man was not consistent in performing his duties. He was unreliable and would turn up whenever he liked. He was also hardly apologetic after such prolonged absences. Solie would give a banal reason for his absence and expect the matter to end there. But where others saw insincerity or arrogance, I saw something else. I'm not sure how to describe exactly what it was that I saw. It simply felt like he belonged to a different breed of men, that he had different reasons from the rest of us. I suppose I felt like this particularly because of what I had learned through Atsa Neiü, an elderly woman who used to be a close neighbour before my family moved to another neighbourhood a few years ago. My mother often called her a human library because of her inexhaustible reserve of stories.

That Atsa Neiü was a gifted story teller is undisputed. And I was perhaps her most faithful listener. She is a few years younger than my grandmother but sometimes it feels as if she has lived a lot longer. She certainly has enough stories to account for it. Atsa Neiü's house was adjacent to ours and I would visit her almost every afternoon. Her husband and sons usually returned home late from work and it would just be me and her sitting beside the fireplace in the kitchen. In between stoking the fire and stirring the pot, she would effortlessly begin her reminiscences while I listened in open mouthed wonder. Her stories never failed to transport me to a different place and time. As I listened to her lilting voice, the background noise of the boisterous neighbourhood children at play outside would grow dimmer and fainter, until it was suddenly just the two of us and the ghosts of the people in her stories which filled the little kitchen room.

Amongst all the innumerable stories and life experiences which Atsa Neiü shared, I especially loved her recollections about her first husband, a supposedly handsome and passionate man who had sacrificed everything to chase a dream of freedom. Encouraged by my rapt attention, she would regale me with accounts of her life with this man who had been the son of a well-to-do farmer. After graduating with excellent grades from a reputed college in Shillong, he had returned home to marry an unimaginably youthful Atsa Neiü. He had also just got a job as a teacher at the Government Primary School in Kohima. An ambitious and bright young man, the future seemed limitless to him. But their life together had unfolded towards the end of the 1950s. Those were troubled times, with the Indian Army occupying the Naga hills and the Naga Army viewing them as illegal occupiers of their land. Hostility grew between the two warring parties and the nationalist spirit, committed to claim a sovereign Nagaland, quickly gained momentum, especially because of the atrocities perpetrated by the Indian army.

It took me a while to connect the pieces of information I had. That old Solie, our office peon, was the same young man in Atsa Neiü's stories. As difficult as it had been to imagine Atsa Neiü as a young girl, it was even harder to grasp that Solie had once been young and in love with a woman, hopelessly in love with a land, indeed that he had ever loved at all! It seemed incomprehensible to reconcile old Solie with the image of the enigmatic young freedom fighter I held in my mind. Yet I know it to be true!

Solie was not one of those men who got swept away by the rushing tsunami of romantic idealism, only to be crushed by harsh reality. No doubt he possessed the idealism of youth, but he was also a pragmatic man. While other men around him, including his own friends and family members, abandoned their jobs or studies to join the Naga movement, Solie remained focussed on the life he had begun to build. Like the rest of the general Naga public, he was supportive of the Naga cause. But Solie considered himself to be more of a sympathetic observer. At the time, as in other parts of Nagaland, their little Naga village was under strict surveillance by the Indian army who had based their camp in the middle of the town area. Anyone caught or even suspected of helping the band of nationalists was subjected to severe torture which, more often than not, resulted in a painful death. This was an effective strategy in setting a chilling example to the rest of the people.

One evening, as Solie and his wife were getting ready to turn in for the night, they heard someone frantically knocking at the back door. Solie cautiously peeped through the window before opening the door. Night visitors were rare because of the strict night curfews. It was Aba, Solie's childhood friend who had disappeared a few months ago. Common knowledge had it that he had gone 'underground', the increasingly common reference to the Naga Army. How he had reached their house undetected by the vigilant night patrollers was a mystery. Solie quickly ushered Aba inside and nervously looked around to see if anyone had seen them, before he closed the door.

Having used up all his energy to reach his friend's door, Aba collapsed on the floor as soon as he knew he was safely inside. Solie hefted his friend onto a wooden bench and asked his wife to bring some leftover rice and pumpkin curry. He possessed an incorrigible sense of humour even under the most inappropriate circumstances. Seeing his friend almost inhale his food without even chewing properly, Solie remarked; 'Hech! My friend! Your body might be dying but it seems your mouth is working perfectly fine!' His wife promptly shushed him in disapproval.

Although still weak, Aba regained some strength the next morning. He apologised for the danger he knew he had placed them in by coming to their house. For some reason, Solie seemed particularly distressed that his friend felt the need to apologise. Aba informed them that he had been sent to deliver some important letters to certain people who were helping their cause. On the way, although he was not detected, he had spotted a convoy of Indian soldiers who were patrolling the area. Stricken at the thought of being caught with incriminating evidence, he quickly dug a hole under a well known Alder tree and buried the letters there. 'I've been hiding in the forest for two days now, waiting for the right time. I can't return without delivering those letters,' Aba said, sounding desperate. That night, Solie disrupted his wife's sleep by tossing and turning in their bed. The next morning, he confided to his wife that he had had a fitful sleep, and was haunted by strange and macabre dreams. And so, after endless debate with himself, Solie said to his friend who was preparing to leave, 'Aba! You could have sought refuge anywhere, but it seems that fate has brought you to me for a reason. Rest assured, I will retrieve the letters and I will deliver them myself. No one will suspect me. As for you, you must return to your group. It is not safe for you here.' Aba opened his mouth to protest and looked as though he was about to refuse, but he did not speak. Instead, seconds ticked by as he studied Solie's unblinking eyes and silently deliberated. Finally, he asked, 'My friend, Solie! Are you sure you are prepared to do this?' Solie nodded.

Aba left that afternoon at a time when people were coming back from work and the roads did not wear the usual deserted look. When Solie asked how he was going to avoid being caught, Aba replied; 'Hou Derei! This soil has borne me. Surely I know my own motherland better than these outsiders?'

Sometimes, Atsa Neiü's voice would wander far off while recollecting intimate memories of her brief life with Solie. I would have to strain my ears to listen during such moments. She would softly murmur to herself, wondering aloud whether deep inside, Solie always knew that a time would come when he would have to make a choice. Once, a faraway look clouded Atsa Neiü's face and she became silent all of a sudden. Unable to contain my curiosity, I prodded, 'And then? Atsa! What happened after that?' Shaken from her reverie by my impatient question, Atsa Neiü first looked at me in a startled manner, as if surprised by my very presence. She then rubbed her face in weary nostalgia and only then, continued her tale in a heavy voice.

Atsa Neiü confessed that she was angry with Solie and sulked for a few days after coming to learn of his promise to Aba. She had come from a family of women who had sacrificed much because of the strong nationalistic fervour of their menfolk. Being the eldest, she was painfully conscious of her mother's struggle to bring up her younger siblings on her own as their father had been inducted into the Naga Army. She had witnessed the repeated humiliation of her mother whenever the Indian Army came to raid their house and subject them to intense interrogation and harassment as well as abuse, both verbal and physical. What had attracted her to Solie was not his unusually fine good looks nor his attractive career prospects. She had been drawn to his complete and utter detachment towards anything remotely political or revolutionary in nature. She was determined never to end up like her mother or aunts. She was a practical woman, Atsa Neiü. As much as she admired the Naga patriots, she did not desire to be married to one.

At first, she hoped that Solie would do this one thing as a favour to his friend and that it would end there. But as time passed, she could not continue to ignore the tell-tale signs, the gradual change in her once content husband.

Solie became restless, often agitated that he was not doing anything meaningful with his life. He started wandering off alone and was evasive whenever she asked him where he had been. She tried to win him over by making efforts to be a more loving wife and ensuring that life at home was as enjoyable as possible. She cooked his favourite meals and attempted to bribe him by presenting joyous visions of the children she would give him. This last tactic backfired as it seemed to make Solie even more troubled. 'One day my son will grow into a man! How will he respect me, knowing that I did not defend our land?' He asked, more to himself than her. Every time information about the latest excess of the Indian Army came to light, Solie would go through a series of moods. At first, he would curse and be angry, then mourn as if he was to blame. Finally, he would become morose, retreat to a corner and brood endlessly. This behaviour incensed his wife and she would shout, 'What pride! Do you actually think that these crimes would have been averted had you been in the Naga Army?'

One late afternoon while returning from the field, Atsa Neiü chanced to meet an elderly woman whose husband was one of the early patriots of the Naga cause. This woman was motherly and affectionate towards her. I remember the strength in Atsa Neiü's voice as she recalled the conviction with which she instinctively understood the reason behind the marked warmth in the woman's attitude. No words needed to be said. Her fears were confirmed. On her way back home, Atsa Neiü thought about the elderly woman's husband, who had been a member of the Naga Club, the first Pan Naga organisation which had been formed during the British occupation of the Naga Hills. Her father, along with this elderly man had together been part of the Naga Hills District Tribal Council (NHDTC), established after the War by the then District Commissioner, Charles Pawsey. The NHDTC did not last as the name was changed to Naga National Council (NNC) in 1946 and the organisation quickly became political in nature after the departure of the British Raj. The NNC soon established its own federal government and formed an army known as the Naga Army.

Atsa Neiü always became very sad while recollecting the later part of her life with Solie. Her voice would tremble and the flow of her story became erratic. She was not a very good story teller then. I would feel incredibly impatient during such times, indignant even, wanting to know everything and frustrated because I felt that she was holding back. This is one of the reasons why I repeatedly begged her to tell me about Solie. The first and foremost reason is simply because he fascinated me. Solie was like no man I had ever known. In the end, Atsa Neiü gradually revealed, bit by bit with each retelling, that she went home to confront her husband, only to have him disclose that he had already made his decision to join the Naga Army. They exchanged bitter words. She told him that she was not willing to be the wife of a dreamer, that he had deceived her by pretending to be someone else and finally, that she wanted a husband beside her to build a life together. Solie simply refused to argue with her and remained adamant about his decision. At one point, she asked him in desperation, 'Why, why do you have to be so selfish! Why can't you be content with what we have? Is chasing after sovereignty really worth risking everything?' A pained look appeared on her husband's face then. A look she had seen before in another's countenance. Solie replied,

'I am not seeking to possess something I never had. I am
running to reclaim what has been taken from me and from
you. We have always been a free people. We were free before
the British Sahibs arrived and subjugated us. They made the
blunder of demarcating and ceding our land as part of Indian
Territory. Don't you see? Freedom is our inheritance!' How
like her father Solie was! She marvelled that she had never
realised exactly how alike they were. She did not tell him
about her own memories although she believed that she was
more intimate to the Naga cause than her husband. For she
had lived under its ideals her whole life. Atsa Neiü's father
was one of the few educated Nagas during his time, having
been taught by the early Christian Missionaries. Through
him, she knew about the various memorandums submitted
to the departing British and incoming Indian Government
on the issue of Naga political sovereignty. She remembered
the heady days of the Naga declaration of independence on
14 August 1947, the 1951 Plebiscite for sovereignty which
was sent to the Prime Minister of India, she recalled the
subsequent collective boycott of the first Government of
India sponsored elections. Only a few years had passed
since but it felt so long ago as those years were her happiest
and final memories with her father. As the political unrest
grew, life became dangerous for the national workers who
quickly went underground. Like many other families, the
Naga cause soon tore Atsa Neiü's father away from his wife
and children. And now like her father, Solie was leaving
her too. She did not try to persuade him to stay or take her
with him. How could she, she asked more to herself than
me, when he was already lost to her. They did not part well,
Solie and Neiü. She once told me that her memory had been

kinder to Solie than she. She then added that politics and war belonged to the men folk and men alone were both heroes and writers of history. I have often pondered over this statement.

Atsa Neiü disclosed that shortly after Solie's departure,she was misinformed that her brave husband expired while on an expedition to China for military training. Still young and believing herself to be a widow, she got married to her present husband. I have heard certain people say that within a year of her first husband's absence, Atsa Neiü began a relationship with her present husband. I never told her this as it would hurt her terribly. In the end, all that anyone can be certain of is that Solie never looked back. Those were turbulent times. In spite of protests by the NNC, the Naga People's Convention, a group formed to end violence and bloodshed in the Naga Hills, held several negotiation talks with the Government of India. These talks led to an agreement called the 16 Point Agreement and in 1963, the Naga Hills became Nagaland, the sixteenth state of the Republic of India. The Naga struggle continued nonetheless. Then, in November of 1975, the historic, 'Shillong Accord' was signed between some representative leaders of the Naga underground organisation and the Government of India. This accord had been signed as Nagaland was under devastating Indian military oppression at the time and many of the villages had begun to starve. The accord brought no peace but instead became quickly controversial. There was widespread criticism and condemnation when the Shillong Accord was signed. Many did not endorse the agreement and felt betrayed. The Shillong Accord broke the once unified Naga National Council (NNC) into different factional groups.

Solie was heartbroken when he learned of the agreement that some of his leaders had signed with the Government of India. Along with numerous other comrades, he vowed to continue fighting for complete and unquestionable sovereignty. The Naga resistance remains to this day, one of the longest political movements in the world. The last people heard about Solie was that in view of his valour and increasing military skills, he was made a Brigadier and had commanded battles against the Indian Army. He had also marched on foot, leading his troops to Pakistan and China numerous times for military training and also to retrieve the much needed arms for the Naga cause.

I always imagined Solie as a faraway hero from a bygone era. So it is with a poignant sadness that this story continues in such a mundane, unheroic manner. It was an ordinary day in the office when an even more ordinary looking man entered, an elderly fellow with a job application for the vacant post of office peon. He seemed offended when asked whether he had quit the underground. 'We are nationalists and will always remain so', he firmly replied. Solie then added that he had applied for the job because he was no longer a young man and his deteriorating health required him to stay closer to home now. No one including I paid him any particular attention. His name, as stated in the letter was Mr. Solie Naga. He lasted for a year and half a month.

Solie hobbled out the office for the last time today. The sight of his hunched and retreating figure depressed me and I averted my eyes. Instead, I focussed my attention on a register that the office maintained, which served as a comprehensive directory of all the employees and their information. I looked up the neat entry: *Shri Solie Naga,*

Peon cum Sweeper. I took out my Add Gel pen and made a tiny insertion of my own.

I wrote: Shri Solie Naga: Peon-cum-sweeper. *And Freedom Fighter.* Nothing changed. All the while, people went about their work. Files coming in, out, keyboards clattering, people sipping bad office tea and gossiping. Living, as if no one ever left.

Remembering Uncle Peter

Today is Uncle Peter's death anniversary. He died, a shadow of the man he had been. It has been seven years since he left. I still remember that long ago July. The phone rang while we were having dinner. I had just turned nine years of age then. 'Whoever it is will call again if it's important', said Mother. Father got up to answer the phone anyway. He spoke in muted tones for the longest time and finally returned with a heavy frown which further magnified the lines on his forehead. 'Peter has cancer,' Father said curtly. Mother responded with something fittingly sympathetic. A distressed Aunt Vivi had rung up to share the ominous news. She said that Uncle Peter had been complaining of pain in his abdomen along with a general weakness and nausea, which occasionally led to vomiting. Uncle had also been losing weight rapidly. There was a small but suspicious swelling on the left side of his neck, just above the collar bone. A biopsy had been done and the results indicated that the growth was cancerous. Further investigation and an MRI scan had ultimately revealed that Uncle Peter had stomach cancer. Father was unusually thoughtful throughout the rest of dinner that evening. I wondered what conflicting emotions were running through his head at that time. He had never hidden his unreserved and blatant contempt for Uncle Peter, who was married to Aunt Vivi, my father's younger sister and the only person in the world Father cares about. Is that an odd remark for his daughter to make? Well, perhaps it is but you shall see that it is not so very strange after all.

Father and Aunt had been brought up by a woman whose name their late mother had given as the closest next of kin in Kohima. The woman had had no choice but to take them in as they were homeless and were as good as orphans. Their father had abandoned them for another woman when they were practically babies and their mother had drunk herself to the grave shortly after. Having grudgingly fulfilled her filial responsibility, she made sure Father and Aunt never forgot their pitiable circumstances. They were treated like the help and made to do all the household chores. It had always been just the two of them. Aunt meant everything to Father and he assumed that it was the same for her. Father was therefore furiously blind sided when a nineteen year old Aunt Vivi eloped with Uncle Peter. The two lovers had met at a trade fair in their neighbourhood. Aunt had been sent to purchase some food at the fair and she had taken the opportunity to browse the stalls which eventually led her to Uncle Peter. Uncle confessed to me that he had been struck by Aunt's beauty and had actually been following her, all the while trying to muster up the courage to talk to her. Aunt Vivi was and still is, a startlingly beautiful woman. She had many admirers. 'She could have been the wife of a big officer', Father often remarked regretfully. This annoyed my mother no end and she would remain cross with him, although never revealing the actual reason why. But I knew. I was the constant shadow in their tangled lives; always watching, silently observing, careful not to take up space I couldn't have. My mother had been pregnant with me long before Father married her. I think he did so only because he was determined not to become his father's son.

No two men could be more unalike than Father and Uncle Peter. While Father is a man filled with terrible longings and a general discontent towards life, Uncle Peter was simply put, a happy man. Uncle comes from a large family with six sisters. Both his parents passed away long ago. He tells me he has fond memories of his childhood. This is not particularly hard to imagine. Uncle's happy upbringing is reflected, justified even, in his blissfully contented demeanour. The many colours of Uncle's human emotions are uncomplicated, without the shadow of a burdened past like Father.

I often felt guilty for being grateful that the relationship between my parents and Aunt Vivi and Uncle Peter was estranged. I revelled in visiting my Aunt and Uncle alone, freed from the palpable tension that my parents would have inevitably brought with them. You see, I was sent back and forth between the two houses to ensure that the fragile bond was not completely severed. I enjoyed visiting my Aunt's house, especially when Uncle Peter was home. Uncle Peter would tell me funny stories and prepare little culinary delights for me in their cosy, well stocked kitchen. My uncle had a knack for making the usual fare appear incredibly special. My favourite was how he prepared wai wai for me. He would first pour boiling hot water over the stiff noodles, cover the steaming bowl with a plate and set it aside to soften. In the meantime, he'd take out the cutting board with a flourish which never failed to send me into fits of childish giggles. I suppose that's why he kept doing it. Hefting me on top of the wide kitchen table, Uncle Peter would present a mock commentary like in TV cook shows, while he julienned an array of vegetables which consistently included onions, and pieces of leftover meat from the previous meal. He would then lightly stir fry the mixture in oil and toss the noodles inside the frying pan last of all. Sometimes, he'd top off the dish with scrambled eggs and add a dash of butter as well. It was heaven.

As young as I had been, I was careful not to reveal to my parents, especially Father, how much I enjoyed visiting my Aunt's residence. I worried that his discerning eyes might discover the actual reason why and prevent further visits. Father conveyed his endorsement of my visits with approving grunts. 'How is Aunt?' he would ask whenever I returned. 'Fine', was my standard response. No further detail about my visit was invited. Father always wore a sour look, as if something thoroughly unpleasant had generously smeared itself around his surroundings. Once, I saw Father transform his grim facial expression into a horribly crooked grin. It was more like a sneer but made him appear ridiculous rather than sinister. I remember this moment well because it was the last time Aunt Vivi visited our house. You see, Aunt and Father had been completely alienated from each other for a long time after she eloped with Uncle. Aunt tried to make amends but Father had resolutely refused to speak to her. Then, he married my mother. Not long after my parents' marriage, Aunt Vivi sent my mother a beautiful Mekhela set as a gift to the newlyweds. Mother adored the gift. This was the slow beginning of a delicate relationship, fraught with a tension which intrigued and puzzled me in equal measure. Of course, this didn't happen overnight. It took years of nagging from Mother for Father to even begin to be curtly civil towards Uncle Peter. He blamed Uncle for ruining his beautiful sister's life by letting her run away with him. Father often derided Uncle Peter's job as a mere office assistant in a private establishment and fumed that he was not good enough for Aunt. Father himself held a modest post in a sleepy government department. I felt that he would have thought this of anyone whom Aunt Vivi married. She was a perfect angel in his eyes. So therefore, I can't help but suspect that Uncle's so called 'lowly' social status was merely an excuse for Father to dislike his brother-in-law. Over the years, I have noticed the scant respect Father displayed towards men with important jobs, the kind of men whom he claims to wish that Aunt had married instead. Father would appear resentful of their success and say foul things behind their backs. 'Hmph! Who does he think he is, some big man, is he?' He'd mutter this to no one in particular and spit on the ground for effect.

Aunt and Uncle did not have any children and doted on me. A pattern gradually formed whereby the two couples met almost every Sunday. Uncle Peter is not particularly close to any of his family members. I heard that his sisters threw a fit when he married Aunt Vivi. There were widely circulated rumours (sparked by his sisters) that Aunt Vivi had allegedly fed Uncle a love potion, thereby tricking him into marrying her. Mother's large family lives in her village which is a good five hours away from where we live. She had come to Kohima in search of work and had found Father instead. I guess we had no one but each other on Sundays.

All the same, how I remember dreading those Sunday gatherings. Aunt behaved too gay, Father hardly spoke and for whatever reasons, Mother's gaze would be fixed upon Father in a steadfast manner. Poor Uncle Peter would try to diffuse the tension by making comments about the food, the weather, ayale! The number of questions he asked to keep the dullest conversation going! His efforts only earned him scornful looks from Father. I wished Uncle Peter would not be so nice to Father. My Uncle couldn't understand that his disregard for Father's obvious contempt only served to further aggravate the tension between them. Then again, sometimes I wondered whether Uncle was aware after all. How very perverse of him then! I would lie awake at night, desperately trying to figure their adult world, struggling to unveil the mystery behind the meaningful glances, the dark looks and pregnant silences, the dynamics of a grown up relationship which was far too multifaceted for me to understand. It seemed that I would be subjected to these excruciating outings week after week.

But then, Aunt Vivi visited alone by herself one day. I'm not sure what transpired. All I know is that Father followed her inside our living room and before long, the two of them began to argue. Father didn't say much but I still remember Aunt's raised voice which was unnaturally high pitched. Aunt Vivi ran out of the house in tears without saying goodbye to me or even thanking Mother for tea. My parents fought bitterly that night. Neither Aunt nor Uncle visited since that day and nor did my parents. For some time, I was utterly content being the only link between them. Until cancer happened to Uncle Peter.

Within a week of discovering that he had cancer, Uncle

underwent a surgery to remove the malignant growth in his stomach at the Naga Hospital in Kohima. Mother and I went to visit him after the operation. On consultation with the doctors, it was revealed that although the surgery had been done, all the tumours could not be removed because the cancer had already spread to other parts of his body. After the surgery, Uncle Peter was advised to start chemotherapy and he meekly gave his consent for the treatment to commence. A few months later, after the treatment had been completed, his doctor confirmed that uncle had not responded well to the chemotherapy. Thereafter, he was advised to be given a course of radiation therapy. As this medical facility is not available in Nagaland, he was referred to Delhi to undergo the procedure and at the same time, to go through more detailed investigation. To finance his expensive medical treatment, Uncle Peter sold the ancestral land which he had inherited from his late parents.

Father had no choice but to come along with me and Mother to visit Uncle Peter the day before they departed for Delhi. It was the first time after that fateful day when Aunt left our house in tears. Uncle sat in his usual lounge chair in the kitchen, which overlooked the entrance of their porch. He was understandably subdued that evening and his fingers uncomfortably gripped the arms of the chair. He wore a faded second-hand chequered golf cap. My parents and Aunt sat around the kitchen fireplace, discussing routine details regarding their imminent trip. Mother and Aunt did most of the talking. At one point, Mother excused herself to use the restroom and this disappearance was followed by a lull of silence. I was relieved when Uncle Peter broke the brief silence by taking off his cap and asking me straight faced; 'So my Anibu! What do you think of my new hairstyle?' Uncle had rarely taken off the cap ever since his treatment began and I discovered that he was completely bald underneath. He said the doctor had warned him about the side effects of chemotherapy which included hair loss and so, he had decided to get it over with himself. I squealed in delighted amusement. An inadvertent chuckle escaped Father and he weakly attempted to disguise it with a cough. Although involuntary, it was nevertheless the friendliest act that Father had ever conceded towards Uncle Peter. Uncle behaved as if nothing out of the ordinary had occurred. He encouraged me to feel the squishy smoothness of his bald pate while I resisted, by tucking my hands underneath my thighs and firmly seating myself on the small crisscrossed cane and plastic mura kept especially for me.

Uncle Peter stayed in Delhi for months together to undergo chemotherapy and radiation treatment. Mother explained that this would make him better and I believed her. Aunt kept in regular correspondence through the phone with my parents during this time. A truce had apparently been called. For once, the murky undercurrents of their relationship were kept aside in the face of Uncle's mortality which now hung in the air. It was on a wistful autumn evening that Aunt Vivi jubilantly rang to inform us that Uncle would be returning home for a short while in between his chemotherapy and radiation treatment. Aunt Vivi ran outside their driveway to greet us the day we visited them after their return from the capital. She seemed optimistic. Uncle Peter was doing well, she said. I ran inside the house, ahead of everyone else.

On meeting my Uncle, I was shocked at the sight of his appearance. He appeared to have aged drastically within these few months of treatment. He had a haggard look and his face wore a greyish pallor. His cheek muscles had lost all elasticity and drooped like that of withered old man Apfusta Zotuo next door. When he saw me at the edge of the doorway, Uncle Peter beckoned me in a raspy voice which sounded more like a harsh whisper. He looked and sounded so different from the adored uncle I remembered that I was suddenly overcome with a combination of shyness and fear. Nevertheless, I obeyed and walked towards him. As I drew closer however, I began to notice the prominent greenish black veins running through his arms and hands, the same arms which used to carry me around. These alien veins proudly protruded, as if someone had inserted thin wires beneath his paper thin skin. I am ashamed to recall that I shrank back in terror and refused to get closer. I stuck close to Mother that entire evening. Later at home, I asked Mother whether Uncle Peter was going to die and she shushed me. The hurt expression on my face must have made her realise that I had not meant to be callous. She then told me that Uncle's less than flattering appearance was only to be expected, considering the gruelling treatment and the added strain of travelling. Fortunately, Uncle began to regain a little colour and looked better in the following days. I was even happier that he seemed to have forgiven me for my earlier appalling behaviour.

I was sent to Aunt's house almost every day after Uncle's return. Mother helped to lighten Aunt Vivi's load by taking turns to prepare his meals. I was their 'delivery girl', at least that's what Uncle Peter called me affectionately whenever I arrived with my hamper. After every meal, Uncle would make me feel useful by asking me to line up his pills in order of size, from the smallest to the biggest, on the bedside table. 'Anibu, are my pills lined and ready?' he would ask, as if the pills' very effectiveness depended upon their order of arrangement. One by one, he'd pop the pills inside his mouth and wash them down with a tall glass of Oral Rehydration Solution (ORS). On good days, when he felt stronger than usual, we'd sit outside the porch under the soothing sunlight. He'd ask me about school and what I wanted to do with my life. I never thought about such grave matters but I told him in excruciating detail anyway. As if I had been planning my future for quite some time. Uncle Peter had a way of making me believe that I could be quite fascinating. It was a feeling I had never experienced with Father or anyone else, for that matter. I felt bold around Uncle. I could ask him anything. Once, I even inquired why he never seemed to mind that Father disliked him so much. Uncle Peter laughed in return. 'Your Father and Aunt, they're unusually close', was all he said. I argued that Aunt Vivi didn't resent my Mother the way Father resented him. 'No she doesn't,' Uncle Peter said agreeably. He then ruffled my hair, lightly pinched my nose and chuckled over my show of affronted dignity. His patronizing brand of evasiveness exasperated me.

Uncle Peter was compelled to postpone his trip to Delhi for continued treatment because he had completely exhausted his finances and was also in debt. He appeared calm but Aunt was always worked up over their financial crises. One afternoon, I overheard Aunt Vivi pleading with Uncle to borrow money from his sisters. Not that they weren't helping already. Uncle's sisters visited him quite a few times after they came to know of his illness. Most times, they came bearing food but every now and then, I'd catch someone subtly slip money into Uncle's hands. Uncle's workplace offered no medical coverage facilities but they had gifted him some money. Other well wishers would occasionally help out too. This gifting money business was interesting. I would never see actual cash exchange hands, just the sliding of palms or a brown envelope being passed on at times. Always inconspicuously conspicuous. Aunt Vivi would be very anxious whenever Uncle's sisters arrived. She never joined in a gathering with her sisters-in-law. She would instead, peep from behind the doorway curtains every now and then, ensuring that all was well. Aunt would take out her best tea cups and serve them the special biscuits kept inside an air tight tin container reserved for special guests only. Once, while clearing up after a group of Uncle's relatives had departed, Aunt became visibly distressed in discovering that a female relative had left her tea untouched. Aunt even sipped the tepid tea to investigate the reason why.

I was glad when my parents decided to financially contribute towards Uncle Peter's medical expenses. When he received the money from them, my uncle tried to tease Father, 'Careful brother in law, I'm beginning to suspect that you might actually care after all.' Father gruffly, but not too unkindly, replied that it was only for Aunt Vivi's sake. Father's comment drew a sharp look from Mother. Aunt Vivi promptly changed the subject by loudly exclaiming over how life had become so expensive and that being sick was a luxury only the rich could afford.

After gathering together some funds, Uncle and Aunt departed for Delhi a second time. It rained heavily the morning they left for Dimapur to catch their afternoon flight. I remember the sky behaving so upset during the early hours of that day, thundering and raging so much that Father speculated whether their flight would be cancelled. Mother insisted that it was an omen. Uncle Peter did not stay in Delhi for long this time. It was as if life was suddenly set on fast forward motion. The turn of events happened so swiftly. After the requisite consultations and investigations, Uncle Peter and Aunt Vivi were compelled to face the fact that Uncle's prognosis was grim. The doctors confirmed that the treatment of radiation and chemotherapy had not been successful. Uncle eventually declared that he was exhausted, both in body and spirit. All he wanted was to return home. This time, their arrival differed vastly from the previous one. There was an air of desolation which no amount of brave cheer could mask. Aunt said being home was like the best medicine for Uncle Peter. Although he did not get better, he seemed to be at peace.

My Aunt Vivi woke with the bitter taste of blood at the back of her throat the morning her husband passed away. Uncle had a special bed in the room adjacent to her but she did not have to check to know that he had already left. It was not yet dawn and a hushed silence filled the room. Aunt Vivi said that the air became eerily still and she could hear her own breathing. Even the soft steady ticking of the wall clock reverberated like dull thuds. Uncle Peter's funeral was a very quiet affair. Our church pastor arrived to pray for the soul of the deceased, although none of us, including my Uncle, ever attended service except on Christmas and New Year's Day. Besides Uncle's sisters and a few other relatives, a group of his office colleagues also came to pay their respects. By evening, Uncle was buried underneath the ground beside the porch where he loved to recline. Father instructed me to stay the night at Aunt's house after everyone had left. I did not want to. Bereft of Uncle's lively presence, even the house seemed to be in mourning. The rooms felt strangely drab and hollow. Aunt's mournful wailing during the funeral had also unnerved me. I started to protest but Mother explained that Aunt was feeling very sad and would feel terribly lonely unless I kept her company that night. I pointedly asked why she and Father could not sleep over as well. This incensed Mother. She boxed my ears tightly while calling me impertinent and sternly told me to do as I am told.

I am sure I woke during the night's deepest birth. The darkness was so vividly black, so overwhelming that I felt suffocated. I covered my head with the blanket and longed for sleep to overcome me. My hand instinctively reached out for Aunt who was supposed to be sleeping beside me. I could only feel the cool emptiness of her absence. It was then, in the midst of my desperate floundering that I heard fragments of Aunt Vivi's voice, broken by fervent sobs. She was crying by herself in a corner of the room. Still scared, I made a little hole with the blanket and looked in the direction of the sound. My eyes had adjusted to the dark a little and I could make out her solid figure sitting on the worn out sofa beside the window. The view overlooked the ground where Uncle was buried. Aunt's legs were folded up onto the sofa and her arms circled her legs in a foetal position while she rocked herself back and forth. It did not occur to me to comfort her. She looked like a small creature in pain and I, I continued to watch in appalled fascination. The memory of this image is imprinted in me. I know I shall never forget her devastating loneliness that night. Aunt kept repeating two words, 'My sins, my sins'. These words were sometimes interjected by another heartfelt word, 'Forgive'. At one point, she kept repeating the words without breath, chanting with such desperation that I was sure she would drown in her private sorrow. I started getting worried and called out to her but she was too cocooned in her grief to hear. I wondered whether my Aunt was going mad. She seemed to have forgotten that Uncle Peter could no longer hear her and called out to him, begging him to forgive her sins. That night never seemed to end. I continued to listen until the next thing I remembered was Mother shaking me awake. It was mid-afternoon.

Things were never the same after Uncle Peter left us. We visited Aunt Vivi regularly during the first few days, making sure that she was all right. She never seemed to want to talk to anyone, especially Father. In fact, she would try and avoid him now. One day, Aunt came to our house and abruptly announced that she was leaving Kohima and relocating elsewhere. She was leasing the house which Uncle Peter had left her, to an Ao family from Mokokchung. Father began to ask where she was going but Mother cut him off by saying; 'Let her go where she pleases'. I was on the floor doing my school homework and stared at Aunt Vivi in distress. I was still fond of her. Aunt picked me up from the floor although I was too old to be carried around. I didn't mind. I realised she was saying goodbye to me. She walked with me around the kitchen garden, asking me what I did that day and made me promise her that I would attend school regularly and study hard. I asked Aunt Vivi whether she was leaving me forever like Uncle Peter and her fair complexion got all flushed as she became emotional. She thanked me for being such a good girl to Uncle Peter. Hearing her say his name made me sob and I became inconsolable. I had been privately mourning for Uncle Peter all the while. Missing dear Uncle Peter was like missing someone who is not mine to miss. I had been suppressing my sorrow as I felt that I could not suddenly profess the intensity of my grief to my parents after he is gone. Not after years of attempting nonchalance while he was alive.

I understand now why Aunt Vivi had to leave us. Father had been in love with her. Mother confessed this to me after I became a little older. She said she realised the depth of his obsession only after they married. Mother believed that her marriage had ended with Uncle Peter's demise. She had actually started to make arrangements to return to her village with me in tow. Then one afternoon, Aunt Vivi paid her a visit while Father was at work and I at school. This was before she announced her departure to all of us. Aunt told Mother that she was leaving town and also mentioned that she would understand if Mother found herself unable to wish her well. Aunt had broken down as she revealed that Uncle Peter had known everything. He knew how she revelled in Father's adoration and how she had encouraged him. Aunt Vivi confessed that she was not the innocent she often pretended to be. Shortly before his demise, Uncle Peter had told her that he was aware of her faults, her vanity, even the lies that she might have told him; but that he forgave her still. He then asked her to leave Father alone, if only for my sake. She was a good woman, he said, and that she ought to know the right thing to do was to give me and Mother the chance we deserved; the chance to have a normal family life. I often wonder why Mother chose to stay on after having her secret fears confirmed by Aunt. But I suppose that's between her and Father.

We never saw or heard from Aunt Vivi after she left. I missed her but her absence mellowed the constant friction between my parents. Life became restful once Mother grew increasingly secure in her marriage. Father remained more or less the same, except that the agitated restlessness gradually disappeared. Sometimes, I see a look in Father's milky eyes. Like a kind of resigned contentment in place of the once unwavering pool of bitter desperation. So much has changed during the seven years since Uncle's demise. Mother is expecting soon. This latest development has brought about a change between my parents, such that I have never seen or could ever have imagined. Father treats her with an awkward tenderness which is as bizarre as it is quite satisfying to see. I still live with unanswered questions. I expect I shall learn more about my family in due course. For now, I am content enough. Yes, quite so.

Sometimes, I take the longer route while coming back from school just so that I can pass by Uncle Peter's grave. I did so again today and noticed a new wreath resting against the headstone. The circle of purple plastic flowers meeting in the centre at the top with a luxuriant bow reminded me that yet another year has passed since Uncle Peter left me. I stood outside the wooden barricade surrounding the marble covered grave and stared, mesmerized, as the ends of the ribbon fluttered in the wind.

Fallen Bird

You loosened your well worn Chiecha and firmly rewound it around your slim waist again. Stray strands of hair had freed themselves from your tight bun and created a dark halo over your head. A few hairpins and a light dusting of powder did little to hide your red-rimmed eyes, swollen nose and your blotchy face. After doing what you could, you stared at the mirror and frowned until your face threatened to contort itself once more. But you were too exhausted to cry and your eyes felt painfully dry. You opened the steel grey Godrej almirah which had been a wedding gift from your maternal uncle and took out some random clothes from the hangers without selection, throwing them inside a brown duffel bag. Unplugging a Nokia phone charger from the power socket, you roughly coiled its cable around your fingers before stuffing it inside your purse. Finally, you stepped outside the porch and trembled, although not from the cold. After locking the door, you dropped the key into the closest flower pot. You were leaving and yet, you only worried that your husband would not be able to locate the house key.

The January fog in Kohima was dense and the winter chill created wispy little blasts of air with every exhalation. The biting cold made you unfold the collar of your second-hand designer jacket as you got inside your white Chevrolet. After warming the car for a few seconds, you drove away from the house in which you had made a home for nine years. You numbly drove past the little paan shops which lined the roadside, each with an impressive telecom company billboard erected on top of shaky roofs, individual signs boldly declaring 'Aircel', 'Vodafone' or some other big cellular network. The names of the modest stalls had faded into oblivion in the face of such powerful advertising. You drove the National Highway, driving until the fog grew thicker and the road ahead became shrouded, like the stretch of gravel and bitumen would give way any moment. This world could end and you would not despair. You still kept driving. You knew this place and it felt oddly serene, like walking down a familiar memory. You passed hills and fields of paddy which have long ceased to captivate you. Your husband used to take you to these fields for little picnics during the courtship years. He was from a different tribe and your parents as well as his had initially had doubts but the two of you were in love, young and brave. You had studied English literature in college and briefly fancied yourself a feminist, empowered and independent. But it wasn't for this reason that you chose to retain your maiden name after marriage. It was because you had never forgotten how an elderly relative had congratulated your parents when Keneisevor, your only brother and youngest sibling was born. 'Finally! a male to carry on the family name and give you pride!' the grave old man who was held in high esteem by the entire community had exclaimed. You were thirteen then and the eldest of four sisters. When you chose to keep your maiden name after marriage, your mother-in-law sniffed and said you were breaking tradition. Even your father disapproved and thought you were dishonoring your husband. Your husband simply indulged you. After a while, it didn't matter to anyone anymore, including you. It didn't make a difference. Your children would not bear your name.

The first quarrel you had with your husband was when you complained over the constant stream of house guests from his village. They would always be somehow related to your husband through a grand aunt's cousin's nephew or some other obscure relation. You didn't like the way they made themselves comfortable inside your kitchen, jabbering away in their language and you felt certain that they were gossiping about you. Your second quarrel was also over language as you wanted to attend your own church on one occasion because you were fed up of listening to the pastor preaching sermons you couldn't understand. But you soon learned the dialect and things became easier from then on.

As you drove, you saw children on the roadside, a little boy who reminded you of your brother, Keneisevor. He would forever remain a little boy to you. You remember how your mother cried with joy that early summer morning when baby Keneisevor was born. Her exhausted face was terribly flushed and her hair greasy with sweat, but you thought she had never looked more radiant as she smiled and held out the infant cradled in her arms for you to see. Your mother had gone into labour the previous night and your father had rushed her to the hospital, leaving you, the eldest, to look after your younger sisters. The next morning, your father came home to take you all to the hospital to see your new brother. There would be no school that day. Your father was in a jubilant mood and took down the detachable covering of your family's soft top Maruti Gypsy which you always begged him to do but which he consented to only during family outings into the woods. On the way to the hospital, your normally reserved father called out to people he knew, while you and your sisters waved at strangers as the sun poured all its gold into the open Gypsy. Father stopped to buy you each TetraPaks of Mango Frooti and Uncle Chips, and glucose powder too, for Mother to mix with water and drink. Surely everyone in Kohima town must have envied your family's glorious undiluted joy that day. You remember the sweet taste of warm liquid Mango and especially the salty stickiness of your fingers from spilled mango juice and salted potato chips. You didn't know yet, that in later years, you would avoid the brightly orange yellow drink you relished so much that day, always condemning it as, 'overly sweet!'

Your parents held a feast as soon as your mother and baby Keneisevor were discharged from the hospital. The senior-most Pastor of your local church arrived to bless the new baby. He prayed so long that you and your sisters giggled and pulled faces at each other. Even some of the adults had their eyes open and simply looked bored. Your grandmother too blessed the event and heartily congratulated Father, which made an Uncle make a joke you didn't quite understand. It must have been very funny because everyone laughed.

Keneisevor cried all the time. You wondered whether baby boys were more difficult to calm down as you had had no problem with Asenuo, your youngest sister, when she was smaller. You don't remember much about baby Keneisevor's life. You only remember too well, the way you felt the day he was born and the day he was taken. It rained so hard during the funeral that someone took a long bamboo pole and poked the makeshift blue tarpaulin, which was collecting excess water in pockets and was in danger of collapsing. Your mother wailed like a deranged woman and clung to the tiny wooden coffin. The women had to literally prise her fingers loose from the coffin when the time came for it to be lowered into the earth. You worried that the box was too small and that Keneisevor wouldn't be able to breathe.

Your mother never fully recovered and your father took to long walks alone into secret places. You became a mother to your sisters. You kept the house spotless, saw to your father's meals, kept him company while he ate and helped him find his clean clothes daily. Things which your mother used to take pride in doing. It embarrassed and angered you sometimes and other times, it simply made you sad. You once admonished your mother, 'Don't forget that you still have three children!' You forgot to include yourself and she didn't correct you either. What you said only made her weep bitterly. Your father reprimanded you and made you apologize. You realized that some people can grieve for a lifetime.

You felt young after a long time when you met your husband. It was a good feeling to be taken care of. You also had a job teaching English at a local school that you enjoyed, but your husband got posted to a different district and you had to resign because you were taught that a wife's place is with her husband. Soon, you had babies to love and a house to call your own. Yet, you missed your family in Kohima and felt happy when your husband got posted back to your hometown. He had worked hard and was a respected officer now. Then one day, you came home to find a woman who informed you that your husband's 'late meetings' were inside a popular restaurant with a woman whom you thought was your friend. He denied everything when you confronted him and you hated the relief you felt because he still cared enough to lie. You hated it even more that he fell in love with you again after he got very sick. Still, you were a devoted wife and stood by him, taking him for treatment and caring for him until his cancer went into remission.

After your husband got better, he took you and the children to a nice resort in a little tourist village for some peace and quiet. It was the first family vacation you had. Your two children, a boy and girl, both loved it. And yet, the resort's history made the place tragic to you. It had originally been a site for a grand supermarket. Unfortunately, the original proprietor had more enthusiasm than business sense and became bankrupt midway during construction, hence bringing the work to a complete halt. Over time, the abandoned half constructed building became a favourite play spot for the village children. It was only in recent years that a dynamic young entrepreneur had the foresight to envision the potential in this forgotten ruin. With the ruthlessness of the ambitious, the incomplete building, signifying another man's unfulfilled dreams was systematically demolished. Within a couple of years' time, a sparkling new resort stood in its place. The much anticipated new establishment was inaugurated during the annual Hornbill Festival. The newspaper advertisement targeted the visiting tourists by proudly declaring it, 'Your Home in Nagaland'.

Memories clamoured for attention as you drove in

silence. You recalled the day your son was born. Your mother experienced a brief spell of renewed life and came to take care of you and your new baby. She cooed and cried over him and you felt like baby Keneisevor had returned. Your mother passed away two years ago. You and your sisters took turns to care for her steadily deteriorating health until the end. But it was you alone who bathed her softly wrinkle spotted body and wiped the excrement and sweat off her mottled bottom when she became bed-ridden and lost control of her bowel movements. Such things which none of your sisters had the stomach to do. Your mother slipped away in the dead of night and did not even say goodbye. She told you none of the loving things which dying parents say to their children before passing away, like the way you see in movies. It was you who made all the funeral arrangements and prepared tea for mourners while your sisters wept over her lifeless body before the burial. People observed it all and remarked that you were made of stronger stuff than your soft-hearted sisters.

You hardly ever sleep well and have permanent bags under your tired eyes. One of your sisters once commented on the benefits of ice cold tea bags for your condition and all you could think of was how ridiculous it all was; her and her silly tea bags, you and this so called life. Nothing moved you anymore. Not your husband, nor your children. You thought about your son and daughter who were nothing like you, although they came from inside you. They were too gay, too happy, always quarrelsome, too thoughtless about everything. No one, including your husband knew who you really were, sometimes not even you. One day, you accidently nicked your thumb while peeling potatoes for dinner and you were strangely intrigued over the cherry red blood that instantly trickled out. The reminder that you still had life flowing inside you felt startling. You neglected to apply a band aid on the cut and instead, sucked your thumb until blood seeped no longer. And so, you waited for life to consume you, just as it had done your mother. Nothing seemed to matter. But then, something other than ordinary came to you a few afternoons ago while you were reading the morning paper after your husband and children had left. A dull thud on the tin roof led you to a bird you had never seen before. This winged creature had a long wooden like beak and was a riot of russet, black and sea green feathers. You thought it might be a migratory bird but that didn't make sense because it wasn't the season. Your bird had no external injuries and appeared fine, but it could not fly anymore. 'Perhaps you no longer want to soar the skies', you whispered in perfect understanding. This bird moved you to tenderness in a way you thought you were no longer capable of. You cupped it gently within the palm of your hands and marvelled over how it closed its eyes with a slow rising of the lower eyelids. You tried feeding it water from a syringe and dug up earthworms from the backyard but your bird refused to eat. You kept grains of rice and cut fruit but your offerings remained untouched. Every day, it simply stared at you with bright black eyes and you felt desperate for it to live. This being knew all your secrets. You wondered whether it saw itself in you just as you saw yourself reflected within its still alert eyes.

Early this morning, you found your bird on the cold floor with eyes half closed and ants crawling over its limp body. It had ultimately starved to death. You wrapped it in a sheet of old newspaper and told no one. You saw your children and husband off and then picked up the bundle of newspaper which was already cold. The chill had begun to spread from within. Kneeling beside the foot of the bed, you stared at your bundle until drops of warm tears fell and dampened the newspaper covering. Today felt like the saddest day you have ever lived through. Finally, you packed a bag, took your bird and drove away, driving aimlessly into the fog.

You parked your car beside a lonely stretch of road overlooking the hills. Cars with people whizzed by as you sat and looked out the window, staring blankly at your own recollections. It was past four o'clock and your children who went for tuitions after school would be on their way home now. You had kept kemenya inside a casserole dish and tea on the pot for them. They always chattered incessantly about their day while eating, not minding that you seemed distracted.

You got out of the comfortable car and walked a bit. Then with the broken branch of a nearby Teguo tree, you dug a tidy hole in the moist earth. And into that carefully created space, you buried your bird with gentle hands. Closing your weary eyes, you found yourself praying for your fallen bird and you had a sudden sense that the words were for you too. It didn't make a difference. You couldn't tell the prayers apart really. Because praying for the bird was like praying for yourself. This small being buried underneath had become a part of you.

You got back inside the car and rested your forehead against the steering wheel. You couldn't remember the last time you had cared enough to pray. You moaned words of desperate hopelessness and longing for things which are not. You released them all and finally whispered, 'Amen'. Although your eyes remained closed, you could feel the warm glow of brilliant twilight hues filling the car. It reminded you of that long ago summer day when it all began. Memories of the sun, sticky mango fingers and echoes of faint laughter came to you all at once. It wasn't all bad, you thought. You turned on the engine and shifted the gear to reverse.

Nigu's Red T Shirt

A pungent, sweet aroma wafted through the ventilator of a dingy rented room in a residential Delhi locality. 'Baiya Nigu is cooking his Naga dish again', exclaimed five year old Rahul knowledgeably, sniffing the air and wrinkling his upturned little nose in distaste. His chubby feet furiously peddled the electric blue tricycle, its shrill bell ringing throughout the entire stretch of corridor as if to ward away any lingering traces of the offensive smell. Curiously enough, the aroma seemed to float in alongside the smell of a cheap men's deodrant. The tenant had clearly tried to mask the smell in vain.

Neingulie heard the commotion outside and anxiously peeped through the keyhole. Mercifully, there was no one to be seen. He had been warned by the landlord not to cook his strong-smelling traditional dishes. This warning had been initiated by complaints from the other tenants who had reported a strange odour emitting from his room. They all proclaimed the smell to be most foul and simply unbearable. 'It's only fermented soya bean and some bamboo shoot', he had stammered when faced with his grumpy landlord. Neingulie wanted to offer the landlord a taste but the stern look on the man's face made him decide against this impulsive thought. He wondered whether people in this city were equipped with a more acute sense of smell. No matter what he did, they would inevitably discover his clandestine gastronomic activities. After the third warning, he had stopped preparing his traditional dishes altogether. It just would not be the same without his favourite indigenous ingredients. But today, he had felt especially homesick and therefore, reckless. And so, out came the pots and pans and the cheap deodorant spray stored especially for such desperate occasions.

Twenty year old Neingulie was pursuing an undergraduate degree course in humanities from a Delhi college. He had also recently discovered that his name had appeared on top of a list which had been posted on his college notice board. The incongruous list was attached below a notification issuing a dire warning to students whose class attendance fell below the minimum percentage required for them to be considered eligible to appear for the upcoming exam. The listed students were strictly warned that they would be barred from taking the exam unless their attendance improved in the next few months. Neingulie had not intended to share this latest development with his academically-minded parents but somehow, they had managed to winkle the news out of him. They always insisted on knowing every minute detail of his daily scholastic life. His doting mother was sympathetic over the phone but his father had been understandably furious. Neingulie tried to defend himself and said; 'They must have made a mistake father! I admit I did bunk some classes but not so many as to be issued a warning.' This only infuriated his father more. 'Why have you been bunking classes at all? And here your poor mother is, bragging about you to everyone at home, about how hardworking you are while there you are bunking classes, doing God knows what!' his father fumed. At the back of his mind, Neingulie knew his father's anger was justified. However, the continued ranting over his assumed insincerity only made him feel defensive and he lashed out; 'Father, it's very easy for you to talk! You don't know what it's like here. I don't have any friends in college and most of the teachers teach only in Hindi. I can't understand a word they say! It's a waste of time even attending their classes.' His father immediately retorted that he should learn the language. 'When in Rome, eh Angulie!' he barked. Neingulie sighed in angry frustration and kneaded the back of his neck with his free hand, an unconscious gesture whenever he felt stressed. He did not bother explaining how his spoken Hindi had considerably improved since arriving in Delhi but that he still continued to struggle when people rattled off the language in rapid conversation, especially during classroom lectures. He could hear his mother's soft voice in the background, pleading with her husband not to be so harsh.

A wave of despairing homesickness hit Neingulie after he ended the call. Hearing his parents' voices from thousands of miles away felt utterly alien in his colourless and sparsely furnished room. He ached for the comforting sight of the familiar colours which he now associated with home. He missed the tidy black and white of his government quarter house, the surrounding yellow and pink cosmos flowers which bloomed in wild scatterings all over his locality. He missed the vivid orangeness of the earth and its towering pine trees which were always slightly damp from the greenest moss. Delhi was so different from home. Everything in this city felt strange; the buildings and its people, the language, food, even the weather. They all served to remind him that he did not belong. The overwhelming heat continued to daze him and he longed for a breath of the crisp hillside air to clear his mind. He recollected in disgusted astonishment how he had once actually begged his parents to allow him to leave his restful life back home. He could not retract his decision now. He knew he had to stick it out and complete his graduation at any cost or otherwise, be deemed a failure. His father had made that clear when he had initially complained about being unable to adjust to his new life. Neingulie had been soundly lectured that his purpose in Delhi was 'only to study and not for pleasure'.

Neingulie was the youngest son born to lower middle class parents in Kohima, the capital district of Nagaland. He had studied at a local establishment till the higher secondary level and had always managed to excel. After he finished his schooling, he observed that quite a few of his friends were planning to seek college admissions in various cities outside of Nagaland. The idea of living in a city for a change seemed terribly appealing and he pleaded with his parents to allow him to study outside as well. He incited his elder siblings who were all married and settled with jobs, to speak to their parents on his behalf. Neingulie had never been so busy as during this period. He was a single minded man with a mission. He had never before stepped outside of the hills which he would learn to miss and appreciate only in time. His parents were not particularly well off and money was always tight in their household. However, they considered their children's education to be a priority. 'Education is an investment,' his father had once stated when an elderly man criticised him by suggesting that he was wasting money through his insistence on sending his children to the best private schools. Ultimately one evening, after months of putting up with Neingulie's relentless pleading and childish sulks, his parents debated the financial aspects, the quality of education and other pros and cons of living in the city. His mother wanted him closer to home but it was his father who convinced her that sending him away was the right decision. 'After all, education must be holistic! What can he learn by being cooped up in this little town all his life? Fending for himself will teach him to be a man.' A few months later, an excited Neingulie left for Delhi with an uncle who was familiar with the city. The week prior to his departure, his elder siblings - three brothers and two sisters – each took the liberty of filling his head with well meaning instructions for surviving the city, regardless that they had never been to the city themselves. They also lined his brand new wallet with pocket money. The morning Neingulie left, his mother sobbed while his father prayed for his safety in unknown lands.

The first thing that hit Neingulie as the train pulled into the station was that Delhi was not the glittering city he had envisioned in his mind. The sea of people, the cacophonic noise and the overbearing heat hit him all at once as he stepped out of the comfortable air conditioned coach. The heat dulled his mind and he moved about clumsily, prompting his uncle to chide him to stay alert. He quickly lifted the luggage and followed his uncle, all the while trying in vain to lose a battalion of child beggars who trailed after him. They poked him and pulled at his shirt relentlessly. They seemed to sense his uncertainty, his quality of newness. It was his street smart uncle who finally shooed them away. Neingulie always regretted that he did not get rid of them himself. He felt that his unceremonious introduction to Delhi's street children sealed the future dynamics of his relationship with them forever. He soon discovered that these midget hecklers managed to zero in on him wherever he went. Before long, Neingulie began carrying a ready supply of coins and loose change in his pockets always. It was his secret shame, the fact that the city's miserable urchins induced more dread than pity in him. With the help of his uncle and some other helpful seniors, he managed to secure admission in a reputed college. His uncle finally left after settling him in a decent rented accommodation.

Neingulie's first day in college began with a round of introductions in class. Everybody had names which were calmly accepted without question. Deepak, Sarika, Priyanka, Sahil and so on. Beautiful names with the precise arrangement of vowels and consonants. When it was his turn, he stood with both hands on the wooden desk and leaned slightly forward. He quickly mumbled his name and added where he was from. To his chagrin, he realised that his voice sounded terribly guttural even to his own ears. The teacher asked him, not unkindly, to repeat himself while some classmates began to titter. The teacher glanced at them in attempted disapproval. He looked at Neingulie sympathetically but his visibly quivering lips gave away the repression of shared mirth. After three repetitions, the teacher asked, clearly emphasising each syllable, 'Ni gu le!

Is that correct?' By now, everyone was laughing openly.
Neingulie miserably nodded, his ears burning, desperate to
answer to any name if only to sit and be ignored. In time, he
came to be referred to as 'Nigu'. He also started introducing
himself as such. It was much less hassle.

One day, while at an impossibly crowded market in
Sarojini Nagar, Neingulie was startled by the sudden and
rude blaring of a bike's horn from behind. Someone shouted
'*Oye chinki! Hato yaar!*' He did not bother to look back
but promptly gave way to whoever was trying to get past.
This place had managed to bring out a quality of meekness
he never knew he possessed. His dignity was slowly being
robbed and he felt helpless to do anything about it. He had
become accustomed to local riff raff and even little children
yelling '*Ching Chong!*' in order to attract his attention
for whatever reason whenever he passed by. This wasn't
something he got used to. It continued to infuriate him every
time. But he had learnt that this was just another thing that
he simply had to endure, like his loneliness. He had accepted
that it was the nature of certain people to be so. As he slipped
inside a narrow alley, he noticed a cartload of second hand
shirts being sold for a fixed price of thirty rupees each. The
owner, a scrawny suntanned man in dhoti squatted on his
haunches beside the cart. The man advertised his wares
by shouting loudly and repeatedly in a high pitched nasal
voice, '*Tisa rupiah, Tisa rupiah, sare Tisa rupiah*'. Neingulie
idly rummaged through the shirts until a bright red T shirt
caught his eye. Both the front and back of the shirt had rows
of Oriental characters vertically written in bold black ink.

Although Neingulie could not decipher what the writing
meant, he felt intrigued by the strange symbols and kept

the shirt aside from the pile. He continued to rummage through the cartload of clothes but could not find anything he preferred better than the red T shirt. Neingulie willingly parted with three worn out ten rupee notes in return for the soft cotton T shirt, now neatly rolled inside an old newspaper. Back in his room, he tried it on and admired himself in the mirror. It was a perfect fit. His fine facial features; the slanted almond eyes, snub nose, his fair but distinctly yellowish tint, the silky straight black hair, they all appeared to belong to his latest apparel. He combed his hair down his forehead like his favourite Korean actor and pretended to speak some gibberish Asian language. Neingulie smiled, winked at his image, gave himself a thumbs up and laughed aloud over his own foolishness.

As tempting as it was, Neingulie did not wear the T shirt to college the next day or to the Delhi Naga Christian Fellowship the following Sunday. Instead, he wore it on a trip to the mall alone. He hardly ever frequented the mall except to catch a movie. Watching movies on the big screen was the one thing he relished about living in the city. However, he did not watch any picture that day. Instead, Neingulie entered a series of random swanky stores and browsed without any intention of buying anything. He experienced a new confidence under the borrowed identity of his T shirt. Salespeople noticed the curiously distinct etchings on his shirt and regarded him like a tourist. On his part, he encouraged their apparent misconception. He did not have to actually say anything. He simply had to wear his new garment like it truly belonged to him in all senses of the word. It was as if he fitted better as a visiting tourist rather than as a geographical misfit. However illusory,

Neingulie experienced a sense of comfort in feeling that there was a justifiable explanation as to why he looked so different from the rest of the country. He was in such an amiable mood that he did not bother to haggle with the auto rickshaw driver who looked at his face and charged him extra, as usual. 'These cheeky rascals!' Neingulie grumbled affectionately as he took out his wallet from the back pocket of his denim jeans.

He wore the shirt frequently after that day. There was always a niggling worry at the back of his mind that he might bump into people who knew him. But despite the mortifying possibility, he still continued to don his red shirt. 'It's just a T shirt like any other,' he reasoned with himself whenever he began to feel like a fraud. At night, he would lie in bed and hold up his shirt like a newspaper, with both hands upright. He studied the curious characters and marvelled that they actually meant something in another part of the world. 'Perhaps this is in Japanese or Chinese, or maybe Korean', he thought to himself. He had initially attempted half-heartedly to Google the meaning on the internet but without results. In time, Neingulie became bolder with every wear. Soon, he was openly wearing the shirt in and around the neighbourhood and had even become more sociable than before. He had also developed certain mannerisms which according to him, were more becoming of his alter persona. For all his new-found bravado however, Neingulie was always careful not to wear the shirt when he knew he would be meeting people from his hometown.

Neingulie woke on a Saturday afternoon sometime around mid-day. His stomach rumbled, reminding him that he had had nothing except a couple of Kingfisher beers since the previous night. He had recently discovered that he quite enjoyed the taste of alcohol. Feeling ravenous, he opened his mini refrigerator which yielded two empty bottles of water, a jar of bamboo shoots, an opened packet of ginger paste and a clove of shrivelled garlic. He extracted a cube of ice from the ice tray and popped it inside his mouth to relieve his parched tongue. Feeling too lethargic to cook, Neingulie decided to visit his favourite Dhaba eatery located near the 'Spoken English Language Institute'. It took a good fifteen minutes to reach the place. As he was crossing the road, he sensed rather than heard, voices directed towards him. It was a group of Asian tourists on the opposite side of the street. Neingulie instantaneously noted that they all wore his T shirt, some in different colours, but the same shirt nevertheless. Although he was yet to uncover the meaning of the writing, he was now well versed with the distinct characters. It was odd, how the familiarity of the symbols was in equal measure to the unfamiliarity of their meaning. The group peered at him curiously and waved with uncertain smiles. It took a few seconds before Neingulie realised that he was still wearing his T shirt from last night. Feeling a little sheepish, he returned their smiles and for a split second, debated turning back. His feet however, seemed to move on their own accord and before he knew it, he was directly facing the group.

No one in the group spoke English but through sporadic words and a series of hand gestures, Neingulie learned that they were tourists from China who were on a sightseeing expedition. He managed to convey that he was not Chinese himself but actually from India. This drew raised eyebrows and laughter. 'Namaste? Namaste?' one of them queried excitedly with his palms joined together in the traditional Indian greeting. Neingulie smiled weakly, unable to explain that he had never used this greeting in this life. He was aware that they were curious about his shirt and struggled to explain how it came to him. He soon gave up in the face of their blank smiles and polite but incomprehensible head nodding. They were a friendly bunch and one of them took out his iphone and gestured for him to take a group picture of them. Neingulie gladly complied. After a few clicks, a young man from the group invited him to be included in the picture as well. The others cheered in response to this suggestion. Neingulie posed alongside the group after handing over his own camera phone to the photographer.

After a series of captures, Neingulie warmly shook hands with each person in the group and they parted ways. Later that night, he smiled as he remembered his unexpectedly pleasant meeting with the Chinese group and took out his phone to admire the photo taken. But there was something amiss with the picture. A feeling of unease took hold and this sudden disgruntlement increased the longer he studied the image. Neingulie was taken aback at how different he appeared from the rest of the group. He did not blend in as perfectly as he had imagined. It bothered him, the feeling that his presence had perhaps spoilt an otherwise splendid picture. Even his expression felt out of place. Everyone's smile seemed to sparkle while his face struggled to fit in. He hoped that his less than flattering appearance was due to the bad lighting in his room and decided to view the picture in the morning instead.

A dismayed Neingulie believed that he appeared even more ghastly in the clear morning light. His face looked like a caricature surrounded by other happy human faces. Disgusted with himself, he decided to calm down by getting out of the room for some fresh air. Neingulie threw on a plain white shirt and took a lingering walk in the nearby park. It was still early morning and the sun had not yet become so cruel with its heat. His leisurely walk quickly turned into a brisk jog and before long, he was sweating profusely. Neingulie realised he had to turn around only when he reached the boundary entrance gate which led to another locality. He had run a considerable length of time and space without intending to do so. He felt immensely weary then. Never had he been as eager to reach the room which had come to signify a place of peace and comfort, however humble, in his adopted city. By the time he reached his building, it was time to get ready for college.

After a long, cold and refreshing bath, Neingulie opened his plastic Burmese made collapsible almirah, brought all the way from Kohima. The red T shirt with the Chinese characters hung precariously on a plastic clothes hanger. He laughed aloud over the realisation that he still did not know what the writing meant. '*Simoderei! N thuo n silietemu ha!*', he exclaimed to himself in a reproving, yet indulgent tone. Without hesitation, he removed the bright red T shirt from the hanger and folded it. He did not have enough hangers for all his shirts and therefore had to be selective of which clothes to hang. He took out a shirt which his mother had gifted him before he left Kohima the first time. Neingulie carefully laid it on the bed. He had never worn the shirt before and noticed for the first time, that she had lovingly embroidered his name on the label. Neingulie then gingerly placed the red T shirt in the clothes compartment which was the least accessible. Somehow, he knew he would not be wearing it again anytime soon.

Promise of Camellias

Camellias in bloom still make me nostalgic. I am reminded of what my life could have been. Sometimes, I wonder whether I should stop growing this soft treasure altogether. It only continues to evoke a tiresome melancholy. But every time I resolve to dig out the plant, something within me hesitates and I can't bring myself to follow through. And so, the bush with the dark glossy leaves and achingly sweet pink flowers still continues to flourish in a corner outside my garden.

Today is the twentieth of November and also my eighth wedding anniversary. My husband dutifully wished me a happy anniversary through a text message early this morning. He's gone to a nearby village to grace some Jubilee programme as Guest of Honour. It does not matter to either of us that we are not together today. He and I barely talk anymore. We remain as polite as any two people can be. As the day came to a close, I filled my watering can and stepped outside. The evocative fragrance of my camellias reminded me of what I have left behind. It was my decision. And yet,

I still long to see his face. Grandmother Sebu was certainly right. One can never get over regrets.

I remember that day like it was yesterday. I had just turned twenty three and naively imagined myself a woman. Grandmother Sebu arrived at our home like a woman with a mission. She is not my actual grandmother but I address her so out of respect. I had been expecting her and peered through the half drawn drapes of my window as she ascended the wooden stairs leading to our patio, located above my room. For some reason, I can still recall the side edge of her Chiecha, which flapped furiously around her legs with each brisk step she took. She and my parents spoke in private for over an hour, after which I was summoned. I knew what the meeting was about. Grandmother Sebu had brought a marriage proposal for me from my husband-to-be's family. They are a very prominent family in our community and my parents were understandably a bit awed with the proposal. Moreover, my prospective husband held an important government post and this created a most favourable impression upon my father. My parents own a modestly successful departmental store. Although we are comfortable enough, money is, more often than not, tight. My parents had given everything to ensure that my elder brother and I receive a decent education. Did I mention that I was twenty three years of age then? I had just finished my post graduation during the early part of that summer. I was also in love with a boy named Theja.

Theja and I had been what people enviously refer to as childhood sweethearts. We grew up in the same locality in Kohima and for the most part, had attended the same school. He was also best friends with my elder brother Jabu.

I remember tagging behind them throughout my young life. At first, the two boys would gang up and bully me. As the years passed, Jabu realised that something had changed when he found himself alone as my tormentor with Theja trying to defend me. He was quite disgusted with his traitor of a friend for a while, but gradually adjusted to the fact that his best friend and little sister liked each other. I often find it amusing how Jabu had not ever acted the protective elder brother when it concerned Theja. I suspect the reason is because his friend played that role splendidly himself. What a remarkable little adult Theja was. Jabu and I fought endlessly over his attention.

Growing up within a small community, being together had been such a natural progression for us. Theja did not ask me to be his girlfriend at any point of time; he did not need to. It was simply understood. I do however, remember the first time that I became shyly aware of our budding relationship. My parents' store was called 'Jabu's', a business very obviously named after my elder brother. My father had established the shop shortly after he was born. At that time, business had started to become increasingly slow due to the rapid mushrooming of new stores which resulted in less of a monopoly for us. In order to boost sales, my father proposed to expand our range of products by selling potted plants as well. My parents were avid gardeners and their new venture became so popular that very soon, Jabu and I were required to help out on weekends and during holidays. I was fourteen then and the boys were only a couple of years older. One summer day, Theja dropped by to help us deliver some potted flowers to the store for sale. We carefully loaded the back of our open top Tata Mobile with colourful blooms of impatiens, petunias, geraniums, and chrysanthemums. There was also a row of camellia cuttings as well as a few saplings, each planted inside disposable plastic cups stuffed with soil. These had been generously donated by an aunt who had an impressive camellia hedge. After loading the vehicle, my father drove while Jabu sat beside him. Theja and I sat behind and kept a cautious watch over the delicate flowerings.

Nodding towards the little green saplings and cuttings, Theja asked, 'Vime, what are these, don't they bloom?'

'Silly Theja, of course they do! These are called camellias and they're still babies!' I replied knowledgeably. To impress him with my knowledge, I added, textbook like, 'Camellias are a kind of woody shrub and some varieties can actually increase in size every year! Auntie Banuo's camellia is almost fifteen feet tall, you know. This plant has a wide range of species and they produce the most elegant flowers, the best part is that they're evergreen. You do know what evergreen means, don't you?' I ended suspiciously. Theja nodded in fascination, apparently oblivious to my childishly condescending tone.

There was an empty packet of camellia seeds nearby with a picture of the rose like flower depicted on the cover. Mother would hang the empty packet over a slim stick of bamboo inserted in the soil, so as to show our customers exactly what they were purchasing. I showed the packet to Theja. He liked it immensely, declaring it his favourite flower. I laughed at his premature enthusiasm.

'You'd be wise to wait and see how they grow first,' I exclaimed

'Who says you can't know when they're young?' he asked.

The way he looked at me as he spoke made me blush. I kept a camellia cutting for myself that day. With Father's help, I replanted my camellia under the shady protection of a tall pine tree outside our backyard. My plant grew at a painfully slow rate. It took years, but I was rewarded for my patient efforts one late autumn when I spied a few pea sized green buds. They soon transformed into glorious blossoms of 'Pink Perfections Camellia Japonica'. And so, on a bleak and frosty winter evening, I proudly presented Theja with a perfect pink bloom.

The years went by like languid summer days, so leisurely and yet so swiftly too. Those were the foolish morning years. We never gave our happiness a second thought. Soon, I had finished my post graduation. Jabu had displayed a keen interest in our expanding family business and Father was already training him to take over the overall management of his namesake store. He would inherit it one day after all. Theja was pursuing a journalism degree in Delhi and I had not seen him for a whole year. He was coming home for Christmas and Jabu and I were looking forward to seeing him soon.

Then Grandmother Sebu arrived with the marriage proposal from my husband's family. Word had already come to us a few weeks ago. My parents had been debating the proposal ever since. My father had initially felt that things were happening a little too fast and remarked that perhaps I was still young.

'Ayale you silly man! For your information, I was Vime's age when I had Jabu', Mother exclaimed in exasperation.

'How old is Vime again?' asked Father nonplussed.

'Twenty three!' Both I and mother replied in unison.

My parents did not want to offend the other family by refusing and were also anxious that I may never get as good an offer in future. I knew my parents would never force me and so, was not too concerned. On the contrary, I remember feeling very flattered. I mentioned Theja but my parents avoided discussing him. They both agreed that Theja was a lovely boy but I was an adult now. It was time to leave childhood indulgences behind.

I nervously entered the living room of my own house like a guest when Grandmother Sebu summoned me. Jabu and I had always been scared of the old woman's tart tongue. Even as adults, Grandmother Sebu had a way of making us feel like naughty little children all over again. She must have asked to speak to me alone because to my horror, my parents tactfully exited the room the moment I entered. Grandmother patted the armchair beside her with her bony fingers and invited me to sit. I could only obey. She then reached out and briefly stroked my cheek. I felt the roughness of her fingertips make a scraping sound as she brushed my skin and tucked a strand of stray hair behind my ear.

'Look at you! A lovely young woman now. I remember when you were a little girl, running wild with the boys, trying your best to keep up with Jabu and Theja.'

I smiled politely, 'Yes Grandmother.'

She proceeded to ask me about my studies, about Jabu and other mundane matters. Then out of the blue, she asked;

'So my dear, I presume your parents have informed you about the proposal. What do you think?'

Although I had expected this, I was still caught unprepared and stammered;

'I, I am of course honoured...'

Grandmother cut me off and continued without waiting for me to finish.

'What is the reason for reluctance on your part? Theja, I suppose?' she asked.

Warmth crept up my neck and spread to my ears. Grandmother looked at me shrewdly and I suddenly felt like a precocious child who foolishly fancied she understood love.

'Let us forget Theja for now; this man, the one who wants to marry you, do you know him?' she asked

'Vaguely', I replied. I did not know my husband on a personal basis but I knew who he was. I knew he was older than me and in his mid-thirties.

'Good! Then you must know that he's a fine man. Mature, good job, good family, what more could you ask for? And he's a generous person too. Someone who can look after not just you but your family as well, God forbid, if anything should ever happen! I know I don't have to remind you that as a woman, you have a responsibility to look after your family. Your best tool to do that is through a good marriage. How long can you expect your poor parents to continue supporting you all through that shop?'

I didn't care for the way grandmother referred to Jabu's as 'that shop', as if our honest little store was something pitiful. I knew we weren't rich by any standards but Grandmother certainly made me feel like my family was poor. That thought had never occurred to me and I suddenly wondered whether other people thought so too.

I was too scared to say anything decisive. I tried to remain evasive, hoping that my parents would rescue me soon. I don't know why but I mumbled that Theja was coming home soon and that I needed to speak to him.

'My dear girl! Please believe me when I say that I only want your happiness. After all, how does whom you marry affect me? I just want you to make the right decision. Has Theja ever spoken to you about marriage?' she asked

I answered honestly. He had not. Grandmother informed me that boys of Theja's age will take years before they even think of settling down and that by the time they're ready, our relationship may not be the same anymore. She asked me what Theja was doing with his life and I told grandmother about his interest in pursuing a career in freelance journalism. Grandmother Sebu was not impressed. According to her, real security only came with a government job. Marrying a man with a government job meant security.

'But what if I became a government officer myself! Then the nature of my husband's job wouldn't matter, would it?' I had sulked.

'Listen to me Vimenuo! As far as girls are concerned, it is better to marry an officer rather than become one', Grandmother Sebu reprimanded me sternly.

To my horror, I became teary eyed. Grandmother's expression immediately softened and she pulled her chair closer towards me so that she was facing me directly. She said to me in an urgent tone;

'Come child! Why are you so sad? I understand that you might feel it impossible to let go of a love you have known since childhood. But who says it has to end? Or that it must culminate in marriage? Theja will always be in your life, no one can take that away from you. Marriage with this man will be a different kind of love. You have been friends with Theja a long time and I know the two of you genuinely care for each other. But you should know that sometimes, we often mistake attachment for love.'

Grandmother went on to tell me about many couples I knew whose marriage she had helped to arrange and how happy they are now. She also stressed what a beautiful thing it was, to marry with the blessings of one's elders. That a girl does not only marry for herself but for the sake of her family's happiness.

Grandmother Sebu urged me; 'I know this man is right for you but I cannot force you. Just remember, a woman's heart changes with time so think wisely. Take it from an old woman who has committed her fair share of mistakes. The one thing in life you can never get over is regret.'

It was surreal, the way everything happened in a daze. My wedding was hastily fixed and I was an engaged woman for three months. Jabu was the one who informed Theja. I tried to call him twice after that but he did not want to speak to me. As the wedding date drew closer, I became extremely sad and would occasionally burst into tears. My mother told me she had experienced pre wedding jitters too. When the invitation cards finally arrived from the printers, it struck me that there could be no turning back now. Mother asked whether I wanted to mail an invitation to Theja. I said yes and told mother I would post it myself. I never did.

Everybody tells me I made a beautiful bride. On my wedding day, I demurely stood beside my groom, covered in white satin from head to toe. And in front of God and man, I promised to love, honour and cherish the man beside me, all the days of my life.

My husband and I did like each other at first. I imagined that fondness would ultimately lead to love. I don't mean to make youth an excuse but, how young we had been! Perhaps we might have, under different circumstances. But we were very different people and we had expectations of each other which were unreasonable, because we were so different. He was an important officer and had frequent visitors. He wanted a sophisticated wife who could play hostess at his regular gatherings, someone he could show off. I remained gauche and uncomfortable even around the help. He loved to talk politics and world affairs while the best I could do was listen politely and feign interest. Perhaps he suffered more disappointment in our marriage because he had more expectations. I tried, I truly did. But after a year or so of being married, I could not stand it any longer. I told him that he could entertain and go out as he pleased. Only, without me. I just wanted to be left home in peace. Everyone, including my in-laws urged us to start a family soon. They said that things would be better once I bore him a child. The final death stroke to our marriage was when we realised we could not have children. Both of us underwent some tests and the doctors mentioned something about my husband's 'insufficient sperm motility'. Although I could not comprehend what that exactly meant, I understood that we could not conceive normally. My husband did not want to discuss our options. It wasn't long before he started his affairs. Looking back, I suppose he didn't have to try too hard. He was a young man, successful and lonely. There was a steady string of pretty young girls. Yes, I knew. I turned a blind eye because strangely enough, I felt a kind of empathy towards him. I know how it feels to be disappointed. It became troublesome when he started flaunting them publicly. He had also started to drink more. My father tried to talk to him once but he would not listen.

Days turned into years and one morning, I found myself waking up alone to my eighth wedding anniversary. Eight years. I marvel at the insignificance of my existence, that such a considerable span of time could have passed even though I have had nothing to do with it. That time chose to go on, uncaring that my life has come to a standstill. As is my usual routine, I walked around the garden to water the plants at dusk. It was then that I noticed something different about my camellias. There was an unusually abundant profusion of buds this winter, so much more than the previous years.

Again, I am reminded that I have not seen Theja for too long. I heard that he travels a lot due to his work as a journalist. I know that Jabu meets up with him whenever he visits Kohima. Funny how our supposedly small town can suddenly be so big after all. We never bump into each other. The last I met Theja was shortly after I got married. My new husband and I were attending a social function and Theja was also there with the local press people. He came up to congratulate both of us and I introduced him to my husband. My husband is aware of what Theja and I had once meant to each other. It does not bother him. I suppose we all have a past. Theja has not married to date and this makes me wonder often, whether he has found someone special. Sometimes, I wish he would just get married. I could take comfort in that finality.

My reverie was abruptly interrupted by the shrill sound of the telephone ringing from inside the house. It was my husband's new personal assistant. He said that my husband

had an important meeting at Dimapur the day after. He
had been directed to inform me that my husband and his
convoy would be travelling directly to Dimapur instead of
stopping unnecessarily at home as they would only have to
leave again in a day's time. I was amused that the assistant
sounded apologetic. He need not have. This is quite normal.
We have a house in Dimapur and my husband stays there
quite often. I know he is rarely alone. I used to feel hurt
and humiliated during the early years, but now I realise it is
more trouble to complain.

'I care too much for you to stay ignorant! Don't you know
tongues are wagging in the office?' sniffed my friend Anuo
'Vime! You must speak to him, put a stop to this.'

Anuo is one of the few childhood friends I have left. Theja
and I used to have a close knit circle of friends. Most of them
felt I had betrayed Theja when I got engaged so suddenly.
I have lost touch with them. I suppose they would have
eventually forgiven me if I had made more of an effort. But I
didn't. It hurt to see them.

Anuo works in the same department as my husband and
has come to help me save my marriage. She informed me
that a woman in their office was trying to take him away from
me. I listened while she related the sordid details to me. I
am no longer the naive girl I used to be. I am aware that my
husband is as guilty as this other woman.

'We could pay her a visit. Women in our clan do that, you
know. It is perfectly justifiable!' suggested Anuo grimly

I firmly rejected her offer although I appreciated her
concern for me. Dear faithful Anuo! How could I tell her that
I did not care anymore who my husband was sleeping with.

'Is she young and beautiful?' I asked calmly.

Anuo mistook my morbid curiosity for jealousy and gleefully answered:

'No, she's much older than us and quite ordinary looking, looks like a cow really!'

I knew then, that my husband had finally fallen in love.

He left me soon after. I cried when my marriage ended. As unhappy as I had been, it was the only kind of marriage I had ever known. I had become attached to my special sadness. People look at me with sympathy, regarding me like a martyr wife. They call my ex husband all kinds of awful names. I thought he was brave to do what I had been too scared to.

My camellias flourished during my first winter as a divorced woman, blooming all throughout spring. Everybody raved about them. I am amazed myself. There has never been this kind of profusion of flowers. It inspired me to plant quite a few cuttings. I decided to make use of my free time by working exclusively as the gardener-cum-florist at my family's plant nursery. I told mother that I would particularly tend the camellias as I was already familiar with this plant. I might have other reasons for choosing this flower but I did not like to admit this even to myself. It seemed too foolish. My brother Jabu has already taken over as the general manager of the store. He had taken the initiative to establish the plant nursery and it had also been his idea to open a separate florist section at Jabu's.

This time round, I was so aware of time, so conscious that another year has passed by. Soon, it would be Christmas again. Early one morning, someone walked in while I was busy sorting out the plants inside the greenhouse at the plant nursery. It was such a lovely dawn. Comforting winter sunlight illuminated the transparent room, giving it an ethereal golden glow while microscopic dust particles, captured by the gleaming sun rays glittered in the atmosphere. I heard his familiar voice before I saw the now matured face. I was glad his voice still sounded the same. It helped to put me at ease. Theja spoke to Jabu for a while and then, came to me. He complimented my flowers and I asked when he got back even though I already knew. He told me that he had been home for a while now. As incredible as it may seem, we managed to get past the initial awkwardness after a few minutes and soon, we were laughing and reminiscing about old times.

Theja looked at my showpiece Pink Perfections mini camellia bush which was full of perfect blooms, each flower with the precise double layers of pink petals so symmetrically arranged to meet at the bud centre. He remarked that he had never seen anything so perfect.

'So Sir, would you like to purchase one?' I teased, speaking to him in my respectful shopkeeper voice.

Theja chuckled and slowly reached out for his wallet while browsing through the wide selection. I made the mistake of assuming that he had pointed to a pot of camellia with the recognizable pink bloom and was crushed when he said, 'No, not the pink one'. He then specifically pointed out a lone flower I had kept aside from the rest. It was a distinctly different breed of camellia. Aside from the familiar glossy leaves, this one had only a single layer of petal and was a vibrant red. I chided myself inwardly. It had been too long! How could I expect him to remember? I took out the potted flower and placed it on the counter, my heart heavy with disappointment. I didn't think he even realised this was also a camellia. Theja took it from my hands, his fingers brushing mine as he did so.

'Thanks Vime. I think our flower deserves a fresh start, don't you?' he said with a radiant grin which made his eyes squint and crinkled the skin around.

For years, I have regretted the way I handled things and have often wondered whether he would ever forgive me. Although it has taken time, I finally understand. I realised that I had underestimated our fine friendship. Perhaps our relationship may never be the same resplendent wonder it once was. Too much has happened since. The past remains irrevocable. But that's okay. Time is enemy and friend too, gathering both regrets and the sublime, into its singular hazy blur.

Bayienuo

She was born around the turn of seasons on a clear spring day in a little rural Naga habitat beside the forest. Her mother Kekhrieleü was a robust village woman who had already borne six sons. A hard worker all her life, Kekhrieleü continued to toil in the paddy fields even during the eighth month of her pregnancy. And it was there in the fields that Kekhrieleü went into premature labour. With no one around to assist her, she somehow managed to find a secluded spot, not so far away from the field area. Lying atop a yielding bed of wild lemon grass with the bitterly aromatic smell of wormwood permeating the air, Kekhrieleü gave birth to a petite baby girl with an unusual abundance of lustrous black hair. The tired but experienced mother cut off the umbilical cord with the sharp edge of a bamboo stick which was commonly known to be naturally sterilised. She then walked towards a nearby brook to clean herself and bathe her bawling baby. The tiny infant gradually calmed down as her mother gently shushed and swaddled her with a shawl.

Kekhrieleü and her husband Medozhalie had been advised

by a health worker at the nearest sub centre not to have any more children. But the couple yearned for a baby girl. 'People keep trying for a boy and you two are going about it the other way!' a village elder had exclaimed in agitated disapproval when he observed that Kekhrieleü was pregnant again. Sentimentalism is frowned upon among the poor. So Kekhrieleü and Medozhalie meekly explained, as they had done during the previous pregnancy as well, 'Ayale! We are grateful to God for blessing us with so many sons. But who will look after us in our old age? Only a girl can give that kind of care.' The old man said nothing but grunted, seemingly appeased by their appropriately practical explanation.

After cleansing and covering her little one, an exhausted Kekhrieleü slumped to the ground and rested her back against an aging oak tree, with her baby safely cradled in her arms. She recalled the past months which had led to this long awaited, blissful moment. Traditional wisdom had it that a small stomach signified a boy and a large one, a girl. Kekhrieleü reminisced over how thrilled she had been when a kindly neighbour had glanced at her burgeoning stomach and commented, 'My friend, how pleasant and feminine you look! This one will certainly be a girl'. All her six sons had each been named by their grandparents. Medozhalie and she had agreed that they would name this baby themselves. They had ultimately decided on two names. If their unborn baby was the girl they ached for, she would be named, 'Mengubeinuo', which translates as 'A child deeply longed for' in Tenyidie dialect. In the event of birthing a boy yet again, he would be named, 'Thejavizo', which means, 'It is still a blessing'. The Angami Naga tribe which Kekhrieleü belonged to, placed great significance on names and an infant is thoughtfully named with the hope that the child will grow up to fulfil the meaning of his or her given name. A name is also meant to reveal the intrinsic nature of its carrier and thus, plays a pivotal role in a person's destiny. Kekhrieleü had deliberated long and hard about her unborn baby's name while she was pregnant.

With her back leaning against the strength of the wizened oak tree, Kekhrieleü looked down and tenderly touched her daughter's delicately pink baby skin with her coarse fingers, hardened by a lifetime of manual labour. 'So you are Mengubeinuo! How long I have waited for you', she whispered lovingly. The unusually peaceful infant in her arms turned her thoughts to the clear spring air and the cries of the cicadas which echoed throughout the forest. It had been a long winter. A honey bee kept buzzing around her head in dizzying circles and Kekhrieleü felt a sudden drowsiness threaten to overcome her. She became acutely aware of the mesmerizing brightness of the soft blue sky above her, a sky that hung so low, illuminating the entire forest in a shimmering way that she had never noticed before. Kekhrieleü saw translucent fairy-like breezes which swivelled around the lush green foliage and blades of grass. She spotted the Hutu flower, blushing and blooming, scattered all over the meadow where she had given birth. Kekhrieleü was embarrassed, she felt the wildflowers had witnessed her most private and vulnerable moment. She forced her distracted gaze back to the tiny infant cradled in her arms and experienced a powerfully maternal love for her baby. While she silently marvelled at the fragile beauty of her daughter's features, a voice seemed to whisper in her ears. Kekhrieleü strained to decipher what the strange voice was whispering so urgently. It seemed to play with her, whispering in one ear and then flitting to the other ear, sounding distant and so close all at once. The voice spoke of springtime with all its glory and urged her to realize how the lovely being in her arms was a child of spring. 'Bayienuo' means 'Spring's Child' in the Tenyidie dialect. The voice was like a softly repetitive echo inside her head. 'Yes, yes, this child must be named Bayienuo. She has heralded spring to me,' Kekhrieleü mumbled sleepily, agreeing with the softly persuasive voice in her ear.

'But I thought we had agreed on the name "Mengubeinuo"!' Medozhalie, her husband, protested.

'I know we did my dear husband. But that was before we saw her. Here, take a deep breath and look at her! Can't you see? Doesn't she look like Bayienuo?' Frustrated with herself for being unable to describe what she had experienced in the forest, Kekhrieleü determinedly placed her exquisite baby in her husband's arms.

Medozhalie cautiously held his feather-light daughter and made silly tender faces at her even though he knew that she could not see him yet. He then conceded, 'Well, I have to admit that her perfect face reminds me of the inside of a cleanly sliced fruit.' He reluctantly tore his gaze away from the baby and said, 'Yes you are right. She does look like Bayienuo'.

Little Bayienuo grew lovelier as each year passed. 'This one will marry early. She has enough beauty for two, make sure her husband is a rich man!' advised Mrs Banuo when the little girl was only five. Bayienuo had suitors coming in to ask for her hand in marriage from the tender age of sixteen. 'We're not asking that she marry our son now. Once she becomes of age is all.' Parents and matchmakers alike would explain when Kekhrieleü and Medozhalie argued that their daughter was a child still. Her loveliness caused her elder brothers to be deeply protective of her.

Young Bayienuo became an enigma to the entire village, including her own family. Kekhrieleü often felt guilty for thinking that Bayienuo was not the daughter that she had imagined and craved for so long. Her daughter bore no physical or characteristic resemblance to herself or her husband, or to anyone else on either side of their family. She had always been very reserved and self sufficient even as a little girl. Often, Kekhrieleü wondered whether her daughter needed a mother at all. Bayienuo seemed detached from everyone who loved her. Although an obedient girl, she preferred solitude and was happiest when left alone. Every day, Bayienuo visited the woods alone after doing her daily chores and returned only at dusk. Not surprisingly, she had few or no friends at all. Bayienuo kept to herself most of the time and had the habit of wandering off alone even when in a group. Kekhrieleü and Medozhalie noticed something odd when their captivating daughter finally reached a marriageable age. There was no suitor at their doorstep. No besotted young man or persuasive matchmakers either. Bayienuo's mystified parents were blissfully unaware that there was an alarming rumour in their little village concerning their daughter. The villagers were beginning to suspect that something was not completely right with Bayienuo. No one could really say exactly at what point this talk began. Perhaps it was triggered by genuine fear, concern or even petty commonplace jealousy, further fuelled by a close knit community's suspicion of unconformist behaviour. No girl or woman in the village could compare with Bayienuo's increasingly blossoming beauty. This caused some of the fairer sex to feel quite resentful. 'Yes, yes, she is breathtakingly stunning and all that. If only she was capable of sitting still and engaging in conversation like a civilised person!' an envious woman might have criticised. The male listener, an admirer of Bayienuo would attempt to engage her in conversation the next time and on failing to catch her attention, be reminded of what had been said about her. Soon, the menfolk, young and old alike, who had all failed to impress Bayienuo, began to agree that their failure was not due to any lapse on their part but because of Bayienuo herself. She was strange. 'Ah! That face stops my heart every time! But there is something about her eyes, a wild restlessness that simply refuses to look at you', someone exclaimed.

There was a more sinister basis for this rumour. Bayienuo's penchant for solitude and her regular visits into the deep woods all alone were beginning to be viewed suspiciously. 'Who does that? I have a strong suspicion that she must be friends with the forest spirits', an elderly woman emphatically stated while the others continued to speculate warily. The level-headed and cautious few maintained that Bayienuo may simply be a little peculiar. But the damage had been done. Just as it was impossible to look at Bayienuo and not be touched by her beauty, it now became impossible to look at her and not think about the disturbing rumours which tainted her. The multitude of the villagers believed that there had to be a downside to such haunting beauty. It was unnatural for any human to be so flawlessly beautiful and just as equally cold and distant at the same time. Atouzo, Bayienuo's eldest brother first learned of the rumour concerning his sister from his wife who had heard it from the womenfolk who sold vegetables on the sides of the road for passing vehicles travelling in between villages. The baseless and slanderous rumour incensed him. 'It's just plain jealousy and nothing else', he exclaimed in disgust. Normally, he wouldn't have bothered with idle gossip but the talk about his sister in the company of forest spirits unsettled him. He decided to inform his mother.

'But you know that's not true,' Bayienuo stammered in distress when her mother and brother told her that she was not to enter the forest alone anymore. Kekhrieleü had nodded in agreement when her son angrily expressed his fury over the rumour which was circulating in their little village. Deep within however, a fearful suspicion which had long been suppressed was re-awakened. Kekhrieleü decided not to tell her husband as the talk would only serve to infuriate him. She had never revealed to him or anyone else about her strange experience in the woods after she had given birth to Bayienuo.

'Whether it's true or not is irrelevant Bayienuo! The point is, you're not a little girl anymore. It doesn't look right for a young woman to wander into the woods as frequently as you do! Do you see any other girl your age doing that? No wonder they think there's something incomplete within you,' exclaimed Atouzo.

'Bayienuo dear, listen to your brother. He has your best interests at heart', advised Kekhrieleü, thoughtfully noting her daughter's reaction.

'You are now an adult and more importantly, a young woman. Your place is to stay home and help Mother around the house. And one more thing Bayienuo, try to make more of an effort to be friendly and make friends with other young people or else they will think that you have become too proud,' admonished Atouzo.

Although Bayienuo had initially protested, she ended her daily sojourns into the woods the moment she realised the extent to which her movements were being observed and accordingly judged. Kekhrieleü was surprised over how easily Bayienuo adjusted to a new routine. She had expected her daughter to put up more of a fight. Bayienuo kept herself consistently occupied with household chores. Kekhrieleü noticed that her daughter worked obsessively and tirelessly, like she needed chores to distract her from other deeper urges. The villagers soon noticed the dramatic change in her. No longer did they see Bayienuo's slender figure entering or exiting the village gate alone. They also noted how Bayienuo never left her mother's side while accompanying her to the field on occasions. More than anything else, the womenfolk began to notice and then appreciate how hardworking she actually was. Seeing the young girl busy at work doing routine activities like cooking, weaving, washing clothes and looking after little children became a common sight. Soon, the villagers began to retract their previous opinion, 'Maybe she's quite all right after all. It was only a restless phase the poor girl went through,' stated someone while the others nodded in agreement. As Bayienuo gradually distanced herself from her nature and drew closer to other young girls her age, a most curious thing occurred. Each girl, on looking closely at Bayienuo, discovered that she was actually quite plain after all. Although still pleasant looking, there was a budding ordinariness about her which no one had noticed before. And they began to accept her all the better for it. When an intrigued visitor from a neighbouring village who had heard of the past rumours surrounding Bayienuo enquired after her, someone from the village answered in a defensive manner 'What nonsense! She's a lovely girl of course, but neither strange nor hauntingly beautiful as you have heard!' 'She's as pretty as the prettiest girl in your village, no more, no less!' Another woman explained charitably. And it was true. Bayienuo's beauty was dimming, so naturally of its own accord that it seemed as if they had imagined the whole thing. 'Perhaps she only had the beauty of a child! The kind that becomes awkward as the person matures,' someone tried to reason wisely.

Shortly after, Bayienuo married and eventually had two children. One evening, as Kekhrieleü was visiting her grandchildren, she could not help but notice for the umpteenth time, that her daughter had not aged well. She searched Bayienuo's features for the beauty that had once overwhelmed her face but could find no trace of it. The villagers had forgotten her past beauty as if it had only been a dream, but how could a mother forget what her daughter had once been? Kekhrieleü wondered how Bayienuo managed to alter her looks and also appeared altogether unchanged. It was in the smallest details, she thought. Her basic features remained the same, but there was a ravaged quality about her. Her skin was no longer luminous, her lips were too tightly drawn and her eyes! Kekhrieleü felt deeply troubled as she observed that Bayienuo's eyes appeared vacant and listless, like a fire that had been put out much too early. That very evening, as Bayienuo rocked her younger child to sleep while sitting beside the fireplace, Kekhrieleü sat opposite and fixed her gaze upon her most unusual daughter. She stared until Bayienuo had no choice but to look up. As a reluctant Bayienuo met her unwavering gaze, a slow and horrified comprehension dawned upon Kekhrieleü.

'This has gone on long enough. You may have fooled everyone in this village and gained their sympathy under the facade of an ordinary and plain looking housewife but not me. Who are you?' Kekhrieleü asked in a tremulous voice.

'I am your daughter Bayienuo.'

Kekhrieleü's shaky laughter held no humour.

'So you keep telling me. Who are you?' she stubbornly persisted. When the rumour had died down years ago, she had comforted herself by thinking that she was simply a foolish old woman, full of superstitious beliefs. At one point, she had even felt ashamed for suspecting such a vile thing about her own daughter. Nevertheless, the fearful doubts had never left her completely. Try as she might, she could never forget how bewitched she had been in the forest.

Bayienuo hummed to her sleeping child and refused to answer.

'I am not leaving this house until you answer me. Imagine what your husband might think if he finds me still here in the morning,' Kekhrieleü whispered.

'I am here because you have named me so,' Bayienuo finally answered.

Kekhrieleü angrily answered, 'All because of a name? Surely there are other children with similar names everywhere. Do you also possess them as well?'

'No. You see, you were the only one who had already named your baby before she was born. But when she finally arrived, you chose to give her to me instead.'

Kekhrieleü got up and walked home in a trancelike

manner. She lay numbed and awake while her husband snored beside her, exhausted after a hard day's labour in the field. She kept looking out the window in mental anguish, urging the sun to make haste and rise from behind the hills. She thought about the daughter she had meant to name Mengubeinuo. She and her husband had prayed about it for so long but ultimately, she had been tricked by a cunning forest spirit. She cried bitterly as the distant wailing of a baby resounded in the background.

And then, she woke up. Kekhrieleü's baby wailed and she instinctively lifted her shirt to feed her infant. Her cheeks were damp with tears and her heart was beating so fast, she could hardly breathe. Immense relief washed over her as her baby suckled contentedly. Kekhrieleü laughed and cried at the same time. It had all been a horrible nightmare! She fed Mengubeinuo for a while and then got ready to walk home. Reaching the well trodden footpath which led to the village, Kekhrieleü turned around and shouted to the forest, 'Her name is Mengubeinuo, the child I have waited so long for'. Just in case.

Mete and the Mist

Sky and earth merged into a blurry mess the fortnight little Mete disappeared. Entire ribbons of distant hills vanished from view along with blue skies and serene sunlight. An unforeseen mist enveloped the peaceful little Naga hamlet. The blanket of fog created a suffocating thickness and impenetrable solidity in the stagnant air, threatening to absorb the hills within its sinister depth. The mist remained abnormally dense and there was a stillness in the atmosphere that almost felt tangible. The village elders gravely pronounced that such weather conditions were unheard of in the middle of March, which was a relatively dry period. An eerie silence permeated the entire village and the villagers viewed this strange phenomenon with wary suspicion.

The doomed search for little Mete was declared unsuccessful. Two long weeks had passed since the little girl's mysterious disappearance. Kevinei-ü, the missing girl's mother, remained inconsolable. The bereaved mother was convinced that her daughter was still alive and lost in the forest. The child had been picking wild raspberries in the nearby woods while her mother was busy working in the field. Now and then, with all the excited energy of a four year old, Mete would run towards her mother with tiny hands carefully clasped together so as to prevent the miniscule orange berries inside her palm from spilling out. Licking her upper lip in intense concentration, Mete would pour the treasured offering on a plantain leaf neatly laid on the ground, not far from where her mother was working. 'Look Apfo!' she called out to her mother, pointing towards the leaf, 'See how much I've collected!' Kevinei-ü responded in indulgent astonishment after each proud proclamation. 'Ayale! How did you manage to pluck so many?' Other times, Kevinei-ü remarked, 'Hou derei! This will do for our dinner tonight'. She was busy ploughing the field and replied without looking up most of the time.

Kevinei-ü was a widow and struggled to provide for her family of two. Her husband had passed away from ill health when Mete was only an infant. The little girl had never known her father. Kevinei-ü made a living by working as hired help in a massive paddy field with rows of terraces beginning all the way from the bottom to the top of a hillock. The field belonged to the wealthiest man in their village. Kevinei-ü was one of his many field workers. In return for her service, she received a daily ration of food for herself and Mete, as well as a modest portion of unhusked rice during harvest time. The owner was a fair man and she had no complaints.

Kevinei-ü grunted steadily and continued tilling her portion of the earth, coaxing the soil to receive seeds before the arrival of the much awaited rain. Soon, the sun began to set, spreading a deep reddish glow across the vast horizon. Kevinei-ü groaned and placed earth-streaked hands against her spine as she straightened her aching back. It would be getting dark soon and it was time to return home. She could see the other workers below, packing their belongings and getting ready to leave. As always, they would wait for each other and return to the village together. As she started to get ready herself, Kevinei-ü heard strains of Thepfhe, being sung by a Peli group. This Peli had already finished their day's field work and were returning to the village, singing the customary Thepfhe on the way. Their voices blended harmoniously, ringing clear and sweet in the forest air. Such singing was believed to wash away the day's weariness and renew strength for another day. Kevinei-ü fondly listened to their song which grew fainter as the young group moved on. She and her late husband had belonged to the same Peli and Kevinei-ü tenderly recalled the many times that they had sung together before they were married.

Shaking free from the wave of nostalgia, Kevinei-ü looked around and shouted, 'Mete! Where are you? Come now child, it's time to leave!' She called out some more times but there was no response. Muttering to herself, Kevinei-ü crossed the terrace field where she was working and entered the nearby woods a few feet away which her daughter regarded as her playground. There was no trace of the little girl. Kevinei-ü was thoroughly exasperated with her daughter. She also felt anxious, knowing that the other workers would be impatiently waiting for the two of them, yet again. This was not the first time that her daughter had strayed in spite of her repeated warnings to stay close by. Confident that the little girl would turn up at any moment as she always did, Kevinei-ü returned to the spot where she had kept her Khorü. As she collected her belongings and placed them inside the Khorü, she noticed Mete's tidy pile of golden raspberries on the ground. The impressive collection of bright berries covered the entire plantain leaf, so much so that the leaf was no longer visible. Unease gripped her as she suddenly realised that the collection of tiny berries was far too many to have been picked by a lone little girl. Kevinei-ü ran back to the forest, this time shouting all the way. She spotted wild raspberry bushes in the woods, dark green and unadorned, without any trace of the familiar orange. It was then that Kevinei-ü actually felt her heart plummet. It was not yet the season for the little berries which her daughter loved.

Alerted by the hysterical screams of a woman in the woods, the other workers swiftly ran up. When they learned of Mete's disappearance, they spread out into the forest, shouting the little girl's name repeatedly. There was only silence in return. There was no chirping, no buzzing either. The forest had never been so quiet as it was that day. Like a woman with a secret. The silence became so intense that Kevinei-ü found it deafening. Soon, darkness began to settle but there was still no sign of Mete. One of the workers suggested that two people could stay back in the field and continue searching while the others returned to the village and informed the rest about the child's disappearance. Kevinei-ü was adamant on staying until her daughter was found. She ended up spending the night in the field.

The distraught mother tried to remain calm but every rustle in the darkness made her jump nervously. Sleep did not come. Instead, a weary Kevinei-ü spent the entire night recalling the earlier part of the day, wishing she had left Mete at home instead of dragging her to the field. If only she had paid more attention to her daughter's activities during the day. She attempted to shake off her morose thoughts and urged herself to be positive. Mete was a brave child and one night in the forest would not harm her. Kevinei-ü vowed that she would give her mischievous daughter a good spanking on her buttocks once she was found. This would serve as a hard but good lesson for Mete, she thought grimly. However, the mystery of the berries threatened to crush her optimism. She had told no one. Kevinei-ü wanted them to have the impression that this was just a simple case of a child wandering too far into the woods and getting lost. Most of the villagers were wary of anything remotely deemed supernatural and may not want to get involved if they knew. She was a poor widow with no social standing and even less influence. Kevinei-ü did not want to take any chances that might compromise her daughter's safe return. She had never felt as helpless as she did then. She thought of her late husband and allowed herself to miss him desperately.

A search party consisting of the menfolk was formed the following morning. They divided themselves into separate groups and spread out into the woods. The men agreed to ululate once in the event of any unexpected problem and twice, if little Mete was found. Not long after the search commenced, someone ululated and then another from a different group, followed by yet another. Each person swore that they saw the figure of a child of around Mete's age prancing in the woods. A young man claimed that he saw a child plucking imaginary berries. The diminutive figure had laughed and scampered away the moment he called out. This time the men, now a little rattled, agreed that they would not signal each other unless Mete was not just seen but held in their arms. They were not prepared for what was to come.

The mist set in almost immediately. It was as if a gargantuan cloud had been hovering above their heads the entire time and had suddenly decided to settle upon them. On alighting, the mist effortlessly spread towards the entire village, darkening the light of day. It became impossible to see anything in the woods with the opaque mist but the men continued, taking pity on Kevinei-ü. They all knew Mete to be an endearing little girl and were genuinely dismayed over her disappearance. Nevertheless, going further into the dense forest increased the risk of getting lost themselves as the mist had greatly compromised their vision. Some of the men attempted to clear the air by waving torches of fire but to no avail. Gradually, they realised how futile it was to keep circling around in the forest, so one of the men suggested that they tie a rope around his waist and keep hold of the opposite end while he entered the deeper part of the woods. He would tug his end of the rope if he required any assistance, he said. This tactic was a complete failure as the rope kept getting tangled and forming itself into baffling knots around bushes and trees.

The mist did not clear nor become lighter the next day, or in the days after. It stubbornly remained still, refusing to budge day after day. Finally, the search for Mete ended on the sixth day. On that last day, the dispirited men no longer searched by calling out her name. Kevinei-ü wept and pleaded with them not to give up. 'I promise you that she is alive and out there! You simply can't see or hear her cries because of this cursed mist!' One of the men had been a good friend of her late husband and assured her that he would personally search for Mete as soon as the fog lifted. Kevinei-ü thanked him but knew that it would be too late by then. The once sleepy little village was now abuzz with a number of theories regarding the mysterious arrival of the mist, inevitably connecting it with poor Mete's disappearance. Plenty of gossip surfaced about Mete and the mist, creating an atmosphere of disquiet amongst the villagers. The rumours ranged from the seemingly logical to unnerving and utterly bizarre conclusions. The only undisputed conclusion was that little Mete was not coming back. The forest had claimed her.

Kevinei-ü sat alone beside the fireplace in her tiny one room hut. Occasionally, she stoked the fire to prevent it from dying. Two weeks had passed since Mete's mysterious disappearance but she was still waiting for the little girl's return. This hope, however bleak, prevented her from realising just how lonely her life had become. She was exhausted. She had not been sleeping at night and dozed off, unaware. Kevinei-ü dreamt that she was in a field just like the one where her daughter had gone missing. She looked around her and spotted a flower with gleaming petals growing on the field terrace directly above the one where she stood. Every time she ran towards the flower, it vanished, only to reappear in the next adjacent terrace. Somehow, she sensed that she was in a dream but this awareness did not deter her from relentlessly chasing after the flower. Kevinei-ü felt that she could not wake up without plucking the flower. In the midst of her steadily increasing despair, she heard a familiar gentle voice, urging her to open her eyes. 'Wake up Kevinei-ü! Go to our daughter at once', the voice whispered. Still, she refused to listen and kept running after the elusive flower which had now materialized at the top of the field. Then for the first time in her life,Kevinei-ü dreamt of rain. Although in a dream, she could feel the chill of light rain fall upon her and the abrupt shift in temperature made her wake with a start. Her cheeks were wet with tears. Feeling like there was no time to lose, Kevinei-ü ran out of the house.

The invisible skies instantaneously began to drizzle as she made her way towards the field, her body determinedly slicing through the endless wall of mist. Soon, the rain was coming down in torrents, just as unexpectedly as the mist had arrived. It was like waking from a deep and restless slumber. Kevinei-ü felt new strength flowing through her as the rain fell against the top of her head, streaming down the rest of her body. With collective preciseness, the translucent drops of water sliced through the hazy atmosphere, clearing the excess moisture suspended in the air. The rain washed away the mist and forced its retreat, effectively wiping every wisp of vapour from the heavens upwards down to the earth below. By the time Kevinei-ü reached the foot of the field, the whole village was sparkling clean and once again, she could see the neighbouring hills surrounding the forest. She ran up the field and towards the forest with renewed hope, knowing that she would not be disappointed this time. And there, Kevinei-ü beheld the sweetest sight lying in wait for her. Tiny Mete was leaning against a tree beside the edge of the woods. On seeing Kevinei-ü, the little girl gave a happy little leap and ran to her sobbing mother who met her on bended knees, oblivious to the slushy rain soaked earth. Mother and daughter embraced under the blessed rain.

Abalie, whose home was near the Kharu[*], proclaimed that even the hardest heart would be moved by the sight of Kevinei-ü joyfully carrying her child and entering Kharu that fateful day. The small village would talk for years to come and then after, about the glorious day when the rain brought Mete home to her mother. Later that night, Kevinei-ü put Mete to sleep after tenderly washing and feeding her. Overwhelmed with gratefulness, she felt no desire to ask questions that night. With the innocence of a child, Mete calmly described to her mother in the coming days, about a towering woman with eyes like smoke who had spirited her into the deepest forest. Whenever she became hungry, the woman fed her the strangest berries and honey, scooped directly from a beehive buzzing with seemingly sedated bees.

Oblivious to her mother's stunned expression, Mete nonchalantly played with a wooden toy and continued in a petulant voice, 'But Apfo! She became terrifying whenever I said I wanted to return home. I didn't like her much after that.' Soon after the change in the woman's behaviour, little Mete witnessed the arrival of a man with tears streaming down his face. 'The man was upset because the woman had taken me and he continued crying until his tears flooded the entire forest. This forced the woman to leave. He then held me by my hand and took me to the edge of the forest and told me to wait for you! Why did you leave without me mother?' Mete ended accusingly. A startled Kevinei-ü realised that her daughter was under the impression that she had been gone for a single day only. Mete was blissfully unaware that she had been missing in the forest for weeks. Kevinei-ü cautiously

---

* Village Gate

replied; 'We searched for you everywhere Mete, your uncle Abalie, Zelhu, Pete, everyone tried to find you.' Pacified that she had not been abandoned, Mete confessed that she had actually seen men in the woods calling her name but that the surrounding mist absorbed the sound of her voice every time she tried to answer. 'They kept going around me and the woman in circles', she sobbed, the trauma slowly building up in retelling her experience. Kevinei-ü hushed Mete and made the now exhausted child lie down on her lap.

Mother tenderly stroked her daughter's soft hair. She couldn't resist from asking one last question, 'Mete, that man you spoke of, what did he look like?' The sleepy child furrowed her forehead in childish concentration and simply replied; 'I don't remember'. Kevinei-ü exhaled deeply, unaware that she had been holding her breath. She closed her eyes in keen disappointment. After a few seconds, Mete yawned and said in a drowsy voice, 'He wore a black shawl, a Lohe just like grandfather Neibou'.

Sunlight boldly streamed inside the little hut through the open doorway and bathed the two tranquil figures on the floor. Mete groaned with the intrusion and Kevinei-ü carefully covered the child's face from the bright light with her shawl. As for her, she turned her face towards the sun and revelled in the dazzling radiance, letting its warmth bathe her fine wrinkles and tired eyes. Kevinei-ü's eyes remained closed in aching reverie. She went back to the day her husband was buried. It was a sunny day and she had wept bitterly, serenaded by the cicada's plaintive cries. She hummed a familiar tune and smiled peacefully, in remembrance of the Lohe with which she had lovingly covered his stiff lifeless body.

The Last Moonrise

Shadows came to life as the luminous moon softly rose behind misty hills. There was no wind and yet, thick bushes rustled. Invisible creatures with bright eyes sounded the beginning of the new moonrise. A lesser known world would take over soon. In the midst of the earth's slow metamorphosis, a looming shadow joyously declared its presence with graceful leaps and bounds. Inch by inch, the owner of this new silhouette stepped out of darkness and into the silver moonlight. It was a majestic male Sambar, indigenous to parts of the little Naga hamlet. His coat was a rich ebony which glowed like burnished amber underneath the serene silver light and his liquid brown eyes brimmed with youthful innocence. The Creator had crowned this gentle creature with a pair of magnificent antlers which gratefully saluted the vast skies.

The forest kingdom had once been as vast. But that was a long time ago. The last few years had witnessed a steady diminishing of forest area as well as its non human inhabitants. The human population was steadily increasing and it was beginning to appear as if there was no longer any space for the other half who belonged as much to the land. This was not spoken of however. The creatures did not cry over the unjustness of it all. They were just glad that the silent half of the day still brought refuge. During this time, the entire forest came alive. The stag never grew weary of each celebration. It was always as delighted as it had been on the very first.

This Sambar had been peacefully dwelling in isolation within the deepest woodland area for years now. The forest was good to him. There was plentiful grass to graze upon as well as a wide variety of foliage, delicious wild berries and bamboo buds. He belonged to the forest and instinctively knew which berries and plants were edible and which could harm him. Nature had taught him well, just as it had done the rest of his vanishing breed. A strange restlessness was building within, as another brand new winter season approached. It had been a long time since he had seen another creature like himself. He stared at his reflection in a clear watering hole which the sparkling rain had recently replenished. He seemed startled, perhaps thinking that some other strange creature was drinking from the other end. His image had long ceased to be familiar. Not that he ever pondered his survival or that of his kind. Simply living each moment was enough.

Tonight, his mounting restlessness was forgotten, for he was looking forward to the new moonrise which promised to be a splendid one. Never before had he seen the dusk so low, a shimmering profusion of violet and orange twilight. The Sambar boldly stepped into the open space, alone and joyful. What a spellbinding sight it was! A magnificent stag gracefully prancing through twilight's meadow with his antlers decked like a crown, welcoming the sacred moonrise.

The moving scenery changed in a split second. It all happened within a single tick of time; the mad scattering in the sprawling mahogany tree, the trembling silence of the forest, the sudden chill in the night's air. Even the moon stilled midrise and hid her face behind the tall willowy trees. But all these were nothing compared to the deafening crack which reverberated throughout the forest. The noise resounded like an obscene echo. In the midst of the mayhem, a tall figure stepped out of the thicket, his right hand gripping a rifle. Slowly and nonchalantly, as if he had nothing to do with the disruption, the man walked towards the fallen animal. The experienced hunter's face wore a satisfied look, instinctively knowing from the moment his finger pulled the trigger, that his bullet had made its mark. As always, his heart quickened in excitement, telling him that the connection has been made. The hunter knelt down to inspect the grievously injured Sambar which was still breathing and grinned in pleasure, estimating that the strapping animal could very well touch three hundred kilograms. He unrolled the rope slung around his waist and proceeded to truss the wounded animal. The stag was hefty and he regretted not bringing his son along for the hunt. He had not expected such a grand kill tonight.

The hunter was a big and strong man, used to the hard life. But he found that he could not even budge the massive animal. He worried that leaving his kill in such a wide open space would attract scavengers. However with no other option available, he reluctantly decided to return home and fetch his unemployed son and some other men to help him carry the animal. He wondered whether it would perhaps be more practical if they butchered the animal into manageable pieces first. Then again, a second look at the beautiful creature made him decide against the impulsive thought. He would show it off first. He knew its exotic meat would fetch a good prize in the market. The hunter gleefully imagined how his bounty would overshadow all the exotic birds and mammals being sold in the market. He would artfully showcase his kill, next to the vendor who sold rows of colourful birds all limp with death and strung on a bamboo stick. This man had hunted enough to know that any species of deer had become a rarity in their area. In fact, no one in their village had spotted a deer for some time now. Another hunter whom he knew well had actually claimed to have shot the last surviving Sambar in their forest. Well this would show his friend, he thought with gleeful anticipation. He marvelled at the sleekness of the dying creature and felt a twinge of regret, however fleeting. He brushed away the uncharacteristic emotion with a shake of his head, as if shooing away a pesky fly. A man needed to make a living, he justified.

He had heard of a preposterous rumour just last week from a relative. His cousin had claimed that some forest rangers had actually seized the wildlife meat being sold by hawkers and had even threatened to lock them up in the event of a second offence. The hunter had also heard that a few village communities in some distant villages had begun to ban hunting in their forests and that this ban was lifted only occasionally. The man gave a derisive snort with this recollection. It made absolutely no sense to him whatsoever. Although he had no formal education, the hunter prided himself on being a reasonable man. The forest land belonged to his clan. Therefore according to him, it mattered not in the least what game he hunted, protected or otherwise. He was glad that his village leaders had not forsaken their ancient ways. Their forefathers had always enjoyed the rich resources of common property. Living off the land's abundant bounty had been their way of life since time immemorial. He indignantly wondered why his generation and his sons' should be denied the same privileges of the land.

The hunter's mind happily revolved around everything he could do with the exotic meat. Perhaps instead of selling it, he could make a trip to Kohima, the capital town, tomorrow and present the head of the animal with its magnificent antlers to the Minister. Surely such a rare offering would find him favour in the eyes of such an important man and furthermore, help cement his son's job application. He wondered which important officer he would honour by presenting the choice meat of the leg. Whistling a merry tune, the hunter walked away, all pity forgotten, unmindful of the majestic creature which had been joyously celebrating a short while ago. Both man and animal were oblivious that something had just happened tonight, that they were significant in something bigger than themselves. There was a sudden shift in the natural world which would only be realised in time.

The quietly dying Sambar lay in the meadow, its warm life blood slowly seeping away, unabsorbed by the cold earth. He was unaware that he would soon become a part of this land's folklore, blissfully innocent that human mothers would regale their children about a regal creature which had once roamed their forest a long time ago. This stag felt no melancholy about his existence, much less over the close of life. With its last shallow breath, a pair of liquid brown eyes gently fixed its gaze upon the moonrise, now high above the skies.

Note: Wildlife in Nagaland is quickly depleting because of deeply rooted native practices and cultural traditions. Hunting is a way of life for the Nagas and we use animals for their meat, believed medicinal values or as a source of economic livelihood. Article 371 A (1) (a) (iv) of the Constitution of India with special provision in respect to the state of Nagaland states that 'Nothwithstanding anything in this constitution; No Act of Parliament in respect of, ownership and transfer of land and its resources, shall apply to the State of Nagaland unless the Legislative Assembly of Nagaland by a resolution so decides.' This provision creates a complex predicament with regard to legally protecting and conserving wildlife in Nagaland, as per National Wildlife Laws. More than 90 per cent of habitual land in Nagaland is privately owned or managed by individual landowners, collective tribal/clan ownership, villages and district councils.

Knowing

They sat across the table from each other. She looked delighted, positively gleeful, while he simply appeared nervous. It showed in the way he kept fidgeting and tapping his right leg continuously. Perhaps it was this contrasting mood that made other diners covertly throw curious glances in their direction. The woman wore a maroon overcoat and bright crimson lipstick. Martha liked how she looked this evening and did not mind the unwarranted attention. The man's name was Ketou and he had been courting her for the better part of the last six months. As old fashioned as the word seems, there was no better definition for the solicitous manner in which he treated her. He was such a gentleman, always so careful not to take any liberties she did not grant previous consent to. Ketou treated her like a fragile porcelain doll, as if she might break with rough handling. He had appeared in her life practically out of nowhere. Martha could not remember the first time she met him. It was as if one day she looked and he happened to be there. Oddly enough, he seemed to be quite familiar with all the members of her family and circle of friends, just as they were with him.

She suspected that her mother was playing a bit at matchmaking and had apparently taken a special liking to this man. She often spotted the two of them whispering and plotting, conspiring like old friends. Under normal circumstances, Martha would have been outraged by her mother's interference in her personal life. This time however, she could not bring herself to mind. He was a nice person and she enjoyed spending time with him. She had increasingly started looking forward to his visits and felt quite dejected on the days he was absent.

The evening was looking promising although it had not begun that way. During the day, her mother had informed her that Ketou had called and asked to take her out for dinner. Martha had been irked by her mother's presumptuousness in assuming that she would have no other plans. She accused her mother of trying to manage her life. If she were honest, she would have admitted that jealousy was the real reason for the sudden and unprecedented harshness towards her mother, because Ketou had not called her instead. Her mother calmly apologised and asked whether she had any alternative plans for the evening. She did not, nor did she wish to invent any.

'The food is taking ages. You'd think our chicken's only just getting hatched,' muttered Ketou. 'Would you like a cup of tea while waiting?'

'Yes,' Martha replied instantly. She was always ready for the comfort offered by a hot steaming cup of tea. Ketou signalled the nearby waiter.

She studied him while he gave their order. He was so

attuned and attentive to her needs. Martha realised with a start that falling in love with this man could be quite effortless indeed. He was nice looking enough, kind, an interesting conversationalist and got along famously with her family. Best of all, he seemed to be really into her. Sometimes, she would sense him scrutinising her intently while he thought she was unaware. If only he knew! Martha felt scalded by his dark gaze upon her at such times and the feeling thrilled her heart. She wondered when he would get down to business and confess his feelings for her. Her woman's instinct told her that he loved her already. Why else would he spend so much of his time with her? Furthermore, she reasoned with herself, her protective mother knew him well and would not encourage the relationship without being assured that it would lead to something genuine. All the same, she needed to hear him say the words. Martha also wondered when he would bring up the issue of marriage. She was thirty five and it was time she got married. 'And here I am, calling my mother presumptuous!' Martha thought wryly. Her amused musings must have showed, for Ketou raised his eyebrows and looked at her in an inquiring manner. They were interrupted by the muted clinking of silverware, signalling that their food had arrived. The appetizing aroma of chicken and bamboo shoot permeated the air around them.

The two ate silently for some time. 'Hungry?' he asked approvingly, noticing the fast vanishing food on her plate. Intending to serve her, he gingerly proceeded to lift a generous cut of smoked chicken with a pair of serving tongs but dropped it halfway before reaching her plate. Ketou muttered under his breath, his clumsiness irritating him, making him feel even more conspicuous. He rubbed the gravy stained tablecloth with his napkin but it only made the stain appear bigger and darker. She looked at him curiously. For some reason, he was especially jittery and ill at ease this evening. He had also been answering her questions in a crisp and abrupt manner which she found to be almost rude. Undeterred, she continued with her volley of sociable queries and became even more determined to draw him out in conversation. She looked at the glint of gold on his ring finger, a ring no different than a wedding band. Martha decided to lighten the mood by teasing him about it.

'So, tell me, really! Are you sure you don't have a wife hidden somewhere?' she asked, slender fingers tossing her loose curls in an exaggerated flip.

He gave a pained expression which she found extremely comical.

Martha continued; 'Okay then. I know that you're a good decent man and I am inclined to believe you when you say there's no one else on the scene. But surely a man like you must have belonged to someone once? What happened? Did she leave you? Oh, tell me you left her!'

He took a gulp of water, 'Really Martha! You don't know what you are saying!'

'Why? Would you rather I thought that instead? At least I am giving you a chance to clear any horrid misconception I might have!' She asked in a cajoling tone. Ketou gave a weak smile but still said nothing. In a giddy mood and refusing to be disheartened by his silence, she exclaimed in a petulant manner, 'Do you find me so shocking?' Her laughter had a tinkling, slightly artificial sound. A carefully modulated feminine laugh which conveyed the supreme confidence of a woman who knows she is admired and can therefore afford to make outrageous statements. She imagined herself a femme fatale, mercilessly flirting, toying with the affections of an ardent admirer. Unfortunately, this admirer was not proving himself to be very ardent tonight.

Try as she might, she could not manage to draw him into her attempted playful conversation. He was so tense and conscious that other people might be eavesdropping on them. It bothered her, this uncompromising side of him. 'What an uptight fellow', she thought. Perhaps he was not as wonderful or as amiable as she had fancied him to be. She decided she did not care much for his company at the moment. Martha sulked and pouted, allowing the evening to continue in stilted conversation. Ketou knew he had hurt her by ignoring her teasing overtures. He awkwardly tried to make amends by scooping a generous helping of white fluffy rice and scraping the flavourful chicken curry off the bottom of the bowl. His efforts backfired miserably. If anything, she found his means of pacification quite pathetic and had to stop herself from telling him so. Martha picked the napkin off her lap and dabbed her fading crimson lips, the rich colour glaringly rubbing off upon the pristine white napkin. He made an effort to stand as she abruptly rose from her chair. He was still eating.

'I'm just going to the restroom', Martha said.

'Should I come?' Ketou asked

'And do what?' she replied frostily.

'Do you know where it is?' he asked with a weary sigh.

Martha stalked off without answering. The evening had been a real disappointment. She wanted to be treated like a woman, yet Ketou persisted in treating her like a difficult child. Ironically enough, she realised that she was behaving just like one and yet, she just could not seem to help herself. 'After all, you become what people expect you to be', she reasoned with herself. The ladies' room was an expansive beige marbled washroom with a row of individual toilet cubicles. Martha entered the cubicle at the furthest end and continued to sit even after relieving herself. She felt no eagerness to return to her dinner companion. The main door swung open suddenly and she heard the chatter and collective clicking of female footsteps entering the restroom. Martha estimated that there must have been about four to five women at least. She decided to wait for them to leave before coming out.

'Did you see them?' a female voice exclaimed in a hushed whisper. There was palpable excitement in the stranger's high pitched tone.

'Asshh! Heartbreaking, simply heartbreaking!' someone replied with a sympathetic clicking of the tongue which Martha found extremely patronizing.

'I had no idea it was that bad! Did you hear the way she was giggling like an infatuated schoolgirl? And the way she's dressed, top to bottom in red! She used to be such a sober woman,' a less sympathetic voice criticised.

'Tell me what really happened! You said you'd explain here', a younger female voice asked plaintively. Martha surmised that the last voice was ignorant about what the others were discussing. Instinct and common sense kicked in, cautioning her that the ongoing discussion somehow involved herself and Ketou. The same instinct urged her to leave immediately. But she could not get her feet to move. A sudden dread overcame her. Facing the unknown faces outside suddenly seemed a terrifying prospect.

A woman answered; 'It happened last year, the accident. She was travelling to some village by taxi when the driver lost control on the slippery kaccha road. The doctors say that the wife's hard blow to the head against the car dashboard caused her amnesia. Traumatic amnesia, they call it. She spent quite a bit of time in the hospital, brief coma and several broken ribs as well. Apparently when she finally regained consciousness, she could recognise everyone inside the Intensive Care Unit, except her own husband. Fancy that!'

Another voice chimed in at this point, 'Imagine! All memory of their marriage wiped clean from her brain. Funnily enough, she could remember people she had met just weeks before the accident. Have you ever heard of such a ridiculous predicament? They had been married a little more than a year when the tragedy occurred. Ketou and Martha, yes I remember their names. I attended their wedding you know!' the voice stated knowledgeably. The last statement was spoken with familial authority.

'I know I sound insensitive but I had to fight the urge to burst out laughing when she started acting coy with him! Poor man! He looked so embarrassed. I wonder where she disappeared to. I didn't see her when we left the hall.'

'Perhaps he's sent her home early. I hear they treat her like a child. They still haven't told her that she is a married woman. It seems they fear that it may be too much of a shock. Presumably it is the husband's idea not to tell her. Idiotic idea if you ask me! Perhaps he wants out.'

'The memory loss is permanent then? By the way,' another woman's voice interrupted in a loud whisper, 'is she quite there? In the head I mean, seeing the way she was acting up....'

Martha had heard enough. She could feel her face burning and there was an alien ringing in her ears.

The sound of flushing water brought a sudden hush to the noisy gossip session. Although in a state of shock, Martha managed to open her cubicle door calmly and stiffly walked towards the exit. She did not care to look at the stunned faces of the women.

Martha was shaking and sobbing incoherently. She passed an astonished waitress or two in the hallway. Unable to face the diners inside, she stepped out of the building, seeking refuge in the surrounding night darkness. She managed to find a quiet spot on a deserted bench under a lone pine tree near the restaurant driveway. She sat there, trying to digest the shattering information she had just witnessed. She knew that everything she heard was all true. Innumerable past incidents which she thought fairly bizarre made complete sense to her now. She realised she was crying only when she felt the cool rush of air evaporating the warm tears streaming down her soft cheeks.

Why had Ketou not revealed that he was her husband, that she was his wife? Was it true that it had been his idea to withhold this information from her? The woman inside the restroom had caustically speculated whether he wanted their marriage to end. Somehow, that cruel statement filled her with more indignation than distress. She felt a fierce desire to protect Ketou from such cynical people. Martha knew with a conviction she couldn't explain, that this was not the reason for his hesitation to reveal the truth to her. She was aware that she had been involved in a car accident almost a year ago and that she had been in a coma briefly. Martha knew that it was possible her family could have withheld certain information in order to protect her. But she had not expected anything of this magnitude. Least of all that she was actually a married woman and that Ketou was her husband. *Ketou*. With a start, Martha remembered that he was still waiting for her inside the restaurant. Without realising what she was doing, Martha unconsciously uttered his name aloud. At first, she felt furious with him. Her immediate impulse was to demand to be driven home immediately. How could he have pretended to be someone else all this time? Who was this man really? In helpless frustration, she whispered his name again, her tongue softly touching teeth on the second syllable. *Ke-tou*. Suddenly the word sounded unbearably intimate. She understood its implications now. Martha mouthed his name again, this time in wonder; quiet and purposeful.

As she pondered over Ketou's decision, a memory came to her. It drifted to her fragmented mind so naturally, as if it had been waiting for this moment all along. She recalled an incident which occurred a few weeks ago when Ketou came to see her. He had brought with him an old photo album containing pictures of himself as a little boy as well as pictures of his late parents and other loved ones. She remembered trying to feign interest as he pointed out faces that mattered to him. 'I want you to know me like I know you', he had told her when she asked why he had brought the photo album. She had given no thought to his words then. Until now.

Martha felt fresh tears brimming, but for different reasons this time. This was why Ketou had not wanted to tell her. He did not want her to feel married to a stranger. Her instincts had been right all along. He was a kind man. And in his kind nature, he had preferred to take the longer route; to allow her the time to get used to the idea of him first. She sat alone in the dark with her thoughts, unaware that time was steadily ticking away. The clear night air had a calming effect and after a while, she managed to gather a modicum of composure.

'Martha, Martha!'

It took a few seconds before she realised that someone was calling her name and that the figure walking towards her with brisk steps was Ketou. Her rapidly beating heart calmed as he came closer. His forehead was furrowed and she could see the relief on his face

'What are you doing here? I've been searching for you everywhere. Why didn't you answer your phone?' He was angry now. Flustered, she rummaged for her cell phone inside her handbag and saw that there were multiple missed calls as well as a frantic sounding message from him. She looked straight into his eyes and exclaimed with as much feeling as she could muster;

'Ketou, I'm sorry for everything I've put you through.'

He quickly became concerned and sat down beside her, reassuring her that he was simply worried for her safety. He gave her a quizzical look before accepting her apology, although he could not be sure what specifically she was apologising for. All Martha wanted was to return home and tell him everything she had experienced in the brief period she was gone. But instead, she found herself offering to accompany him inside the restaurant again. He had not taken care of the bill yet.

Once they reached their table, Martha knew she could not bear to let their evening end this way. It was for his sake that she felt a desperate need to give their outing a dignified finish. She studied his face. His eyes looked tired and he no longer seemed to care about the curious glances.

'Actually I wouldn't mind some dessert, that is, if you'd like some?' She asked tentatively, bracing herself for a possibly negative answer. She would understand if he did not want to linger.

'Are you sure?' he asked.

She nodded

Once again, they sat across the table from each other, a husband and a wife. They each had a crystal bowl containing something sweet, which they appeared to be relishing. The woman wore a maroon coat and looked radiant. He appeared a tad flustered but happy nevertheless. He raised his eyebrows in a gesture of enquiry as she warmly smiled at him across the table. For now, she only gave him a knowing look.

Dielienuo's Choice

Dielienuo entered my life shortly after my parents announced that I was getting a baby brother. Mother tenderly rubbed her stomach as she sat me down to explain that he was still inside her tummy, just as I had been before I came into the world. My initial reaction to this news was insecurity. I had been the centre of my parents' world for too long; ten glorious years. I wondered whether this new addition would affect my standing in the family and worried that they might love me less. However as time passed, I became increasingly excited at the prospect of becoming somebody's elder sister. I must admit that there have been times when I experienced envy towards my cousins who had younger siblings. They would act all grown up and bossy, even towards me. This was in spite of the fact that we were the same age. I suppose being older than someone else in the family does tend to make one appear more grown up somehow.

Mother's stomach steadily grew bigger as the months passed and she began to pad around the house barefoot a lot, something she never allows me to do. Mother is a housewife and my father, a busy doctor who works at the local hospital. As Mother's pregnancy advanced, housework became problematic and she also began to feel unwell quite often. This was when my parents started to discuss the practicality of hiring a live-in maid to help out around the house. They asked around a lot but could not find anyone suitable. Then one afternoon, my father informed me that besides getting a baby brother, I would also be getting a new friend. Father explained that there was a poor family in one of the more remote Naga villages who was struggling to make ends meet. My parents had therefore, agreed to take in one of the children, who was the same age as me. This girl would help Mother around the house and in return, my parents would send her to school and also dispatch money to her family every month. Her name was Dielienuo.

I first saw Dielienuo timidly sitting on a small mura beside her uncle who had brought her from the village. I had come home from school to find Mother conversing with Dielienuo's uncle inside our kitchen which always smelled divine, courtesy of the aroma of smoked meat hanging above the fireplace. Dielienuo seemed sad but did not cry when her uncle left. He was her maternal aunt's husband. We learned that both Dielienuo's biological parents had passed away when she was very young and her Aunt and Uncle had taken her in thereafter. After her uncle left, Mother showed Dielienuo where she would be sleeping. We did not have extra rooms but there was a small storage space between the kitchen and the corridor which led to the other rooms. Mother cleared the space and Father installed a bed for Dielienuo. I noticed to my immense astonishment that she had not brought any luggage. She only had with her, a polythene bag containing two tattered pieces of clothing and an over ripe banana, more black than yellow, obviously meant to be consumed much earlier. After inspecting her meagre belongings, mother gave her some of my hand-me-downs to wear. Although we were the same age, my clothes hung on her painfully emaciated frame. In time, Dielienuo slowly filled out, thanks to my mother's solid meals. My parents were initially a little apprehensive about the language barrier. Hence, they were pleasantly surprised to discover that Dielienuo could speak Nagamese, the common Naga lingua franca. Contrary to what my parents had assumed, Dielienuo was not completely new to the urban areas. Her uncle revealed that she had worked for some time in the household of an elderly lady in Dimapur district. He further explained that Dielienuo had been miserable there and so, he had taken her back to their village. He said this with an air of magnanimity, conscious of his act of compassion towards a little girl under his care. However, poverty had compelled them to send her away a second time, this time to us.

Dielienuo didn't talk much. She would quietly do the chores assigned to her by mother. Every evening after washing the dishes, she would go to the back of the house and sit outside our bamboo sadze, an extended platform stretching away from the ground. Suspended in mid air, Dielienuo would watch the starlit Kohima sky. She was always so calm and mature that I wondered whether she ever did such a childish thing like missing her family. Early one morning, as I sleepily walked towards the kitchen for a glass of water, I could smell the stench of urine wafting out from the mattress where Dielienuo slept. She had wet her bed. I found out that Dielienuo had been wetting her bed regularly ever since she arrived. My exasperated mother finally had to cover her mattress with a plastic sheet. When mother learned that I was aware of the situation, she sat me down and warned me not to tease Dielienuo and suggested that I should try to befriend her instead as she was obviously very lonely and homesick. Mother had read that bed wetting by older children was commonly due to psychological stress and trauma, possibly caused by sudden transitions in life. My awe of Dielienuo disappeared with this revelation and I reached out to her that evening. At first, she appeared a little wary of my sudden friendliness but I wore her down fast. We were still little girls after all and soon, we were chatting animatedly. We sat underneath the stars and spoke about inconsequential things which didn't matter as much as the fact that we were saying them to each other. Finally, mother called us in as it was time for bed.

Dielienuo and I became grand friends soon. Since she had arrived at an odd time when school admissions were already over, my parents decided to send her to school during the next academic year instead. I enjoyed playing with Dielienuo more than anyone else. She was always so sweet and agreeable, pandering to my every whim as if her very survival depended on my happiness. I looked forward to coming home from school, knowing that Dielienuo would be waiting for me. We would play kitchen, dress up and play an exhausting series of hand games which involved a lot of synchronised clapping and nonsensical rhymes. Sometimes Mother would complain that I was keeping Dielienuo away from her chores but I don't think she minded all that much, now that I no longer pestered her by complaining of boredom. Father always came home from work late and since there were no neighbourhood children my age, it was mostly always mother and I alone.

I began to have a sense that my friendship with Dielienuo was different from the usual. There was an underlying unease which quietly grew alongside our budding friendship. It seemed that this perplexing feeling steadily increased the more I grew to love her. There were times I felt terribly guilty although I could not exactly comprehend the reason why. Such times as when we would be two little girls playing with my Barbie dolls one ordinary night and the next morning, I would wake up sleepily in my pyjamas to see her scrubbing the floor on her knees. Perhaps I chose to remain ignorant. Dielienuo always had to wake up at the crack of dawn, even on weekends and other holidays, even the coldest winter mornings too. She loved to watch cartoons on television and would squeal in delight over kiddie serials which I myself have outgrown. Whenever mother called her midway during such a programme, she would answer very reluctantly with her eyes still glued to the screen. Mother would then storm over and switch off the television herself, bringing the programme to an abrupt end. Dielienuo was also always in awe of my ten year old's possessions. 'Are all these yours?' she had reverently whispered when she entered my room for the first time, browsing through my playthings and my many clothes in open-mouthed bewilderment. My initial pride over Dielienuo's wonder at my material belongings wore off swiftly. In time, I did not want her inside my room. Her unflagging admiration not only irritated but shamed me as well.

It wasn't mine but Dielienuo's life which changed with the birth of my baby brother. She was the busiest ten-year old I have ever seen. She would hover over him constantly, looking after him, carrying and mothering him. Seeing Dielienuo slightly hunched to the right with the weight of a large duffel bag stuffed with my brother's baby essentials became a common sight during family outings. But sometimes, while my baby brother was asleep, Dielienuo was free to be my friend again. And in spite of everything that was happening around us, our friendship miraculously seemed to remain intact.

Time went on and soon, my eleventh birthday approached. Turning eleven felt no different from being ten, but my parents obviously thought otherwise and made quite a fuss over me. They decided to throw a gala birthday bash in my honour. All my cousins from both the paternal and maternal side of my family as well as a few friends from school were invited. I had been feeling a tad sidelined by my parents ever since the arrival of my baby brother and this party almost seemed to make up for it. Mother even ordered a special pink birthday cake with candles and allowed me to choose the sweet treats to give away as party favours. Poor Dielienuo was bewildered. She could not understand the concept of a birthday party. 'So your parents celebrate the day you were born every year? Why?' she asked in a tone that conveyed part amazement as well as a little scorn. I realised that Dielienuo had never been wished on her birthday, let alone had a birthday celebrated. I asked her when her birthday was and she pointed to a number on the wall calendar rather randomly. I was sure she did not know when her birthday was. In fact, I began to doubt whether she even knew her actual age at all. I was allowed to miss school on my birthday. I watched cartoons on television while

Mother and Dielienuo kept busy the entire day, preparing for my evening party.

'Who's that?' a friend whispered in my ear, pointing towards Dielienuo who was serving black tea to the adults in a huge tray. Everyone had already eaten then. I looked at Dielienuo's dishevelled hair and second-hand dress which was spotted with the scrumptious food she had helped mother to prepare. I knew she had been working the whole day on my account. This knowledge could not prevent me from being ashamed of her. Seeing Dielienuo's pitiable appearance beside my friends in their clean clothes and bright faces mortified me. 'Oh, she's just a servant', I replied airily. Later, while we were indulging in some party games, Father encouraged me to include Dielienuo as well. I found her inside the kitchen, scraping leftovers off the plates, keeping aside the bones for our pet Alsatian Teizei, just as she had been taught. Dielienuo refused to join us, claiming that she had too much work to do. I knew that Mother would not mind if I took her away but I did not insist. I was in fact, relieved, that she had declined.

Dielienuo reverted to her old reserved self ever since my eleventh birthday. She was always busy, either with my baby brother or some other housework. She never wanted to play anymore. It was ironic that my birthday had aged her into a little adult. Dielienuo was never rude to me. She just had other things to attend to. At first I was convinced that she was ignoring me on purpose. I anxiously worried whether she had possibly heard me dismiss her so nonchalantly that night and imagined that she had recognised the relief on my face because she had not behaved familiarly as she passed by me and my curious friends. I was so sure she was punishing me. But the weeks turned into months without any sign of outburst from her and finally, I had to accept that Dielienuo was no longer the little girl I still was. After some time, I stopped asking her to play with me.

One late evening, Father came home from work in an extremely disturbed mood. He sat on his usual chair beside the dining table and related his day's experience while Mother warmed his food. A twelve-year old non local boy had been brought to the hospital where Father worked. The boy was a domestic help and had been repeatedly subjected to physical abuse by a male relative of his employers. The employer himself had brought the boy to the hospital. He claimed to have no knowledge of what had been transpiring in his own house and said that he had only just discovered the boy's latest injury and had therefore, immediately brought him to the hospital. Although agreeing to submit the boy under the care of a local NGO, the employer refused to press charges against the perpetrator as he was a close relative. Father said that the young boy had been staying with his employers for years now and did not remember anything about his biological family or about his past. He only vaguely recalled that a woman known to his parents had brought him to his employer's house a long time ago. He had been working there ever since. Father remarked that the chances of this boy being repatriated to his family were bleak. I found myself asking what 'repatriated' meant. Father swiftly turned around at the sound of my voice and realised that Dielienuo and I were intently listening to his story. He had been too engrossed to notice our little figures sitting beside the kitchen fire place. Father scolded mother for letting us stay up so late even though it was still early. Realising that he was in a tense mood, Mother quickly shooed us away from the kitchen, telling us that this conversation was not appropriate for 'little ears'. I followed Dielienuo outside our sadze where she always sat during the evening after finishing her chores. I wanted to discuss what we had heard but Dielienuo remained very quiet the entire time. After a while, I got bored and left Dielienuo to her nightly stargazing.

Dielienuo's uncle arrived on a lazy Sunday afternoon to take her home for their annual village Christmas celebration. He had rung Father from Dimapur district two days before and informed him that he would be coming to collect her. Dielienuo had been with us for almost two years now and was also attending the government primary school located near our house. Father took Dielienuo's uncle aside after he arrived and the two men conversed while Mother helped Dielienuo pack her essentials. Mother included a blanket and some hand-me-down clothes for the rest of Dielienuo's family. She had come to us with nothing but mother ensured that she was going home with a lot more material possessions, if nothing else. After some time, Father and Dielienuo's Uncle emerged and summoned Dielienuo. The latter looked her over and merrily commented on her weight gain. Glancing at her conspicuous new luggage, he instructed Dielienuo to say thank you to mother and added that he would bring her back soon. Dielienuo obediently thanked mother in a small voice but remained sullen otherwise. I couldn't make out whether she was excited to be going home at all. Father answered that as much as we were helped by Dielienuo's services, she should come back only if she wanted to. Her uncle laughed at father's remark and asked how any sane person would not want to return to a house with facilities that were non-existent in their village. 'Running water, good food, school, new clothes, *Aru ki lage*?' he asked rather crudely. A look of irritation crossed Father's face but he ignored the man's presumptuous remark and determinedly looked at Dielienuo, encouraging her to speak up for herself. Father then impulsively asked Dielienuo to sit down. He glanced towards Dielienuo's uncle, as if wishing the man away and suggested that Mother prepare another cup of tea for him. Taking the hint, mother made casual conversation with Dielienuo's uncle while leading him away towards the kitchen. I could hear my mother genially asking the man whether he would like some food packed for himself and Dielienuo to have on the journey. Father kneeled in front of a timid Dielienuo and gently asked whether she was happy and if she wanted to come back to stay with us. Dielienuo looked stunned. It was apparent that she had never been asked for an opinion about her own life. Dielienuo fidgeted for some time, wringing her hands and looking down her sandaled feet. Finally, she looked up and whispered, 'I'll only be sent somewhere else'.

Dielienuo returned after a month's stay at her village. I found myself a little more indifferent towards her arrival than I would have expected. I was of course, glad to have her back. But I could no longer greet her arrival like that of a cherished friend. We were growing up and with it, our relationship. Nevertheless, I still joined her underneath the stars on the first night of her return. We sat in silence for a while. I asked, without much mulling, 'Do you watch the stars when you're home as well?' She smiled, clearly pleased with my question; 'Yes, every night. And do you know? They're the same everywhere I go'. Dielienuo did not look at me when she replied. She had a faraway look, her tone, reassuring no one but herself.

That Long Ago Summer

Do you remember? That long ago summer day? How our heads rested against the grass, pliant and sprinkled with tiny purple wildflowers. I was finicky at first, not wanting to ruin my temporary curls, the result of sleeping with braided hair the previous night. But you were so sweet, so charming, lending me your best Sunday jacket to pillow my head. You offered it with such lazy nonchalance, oblivious to the awakening of that young heart lying next to you. We lay side by side, so close that I could see the skin around your eyes crinkle as you squinted against the blinding glare of the white sky. And when you turned to say something, I felt overcome with shyness. I had never seen your face this close to mine. You had a brown freckle underneath the curve of your lower lip.

I had just turned fourteen then and you, seventeen perhaps?

We were abruptly interrupted. I could hear mother shouting my name from inside your house, hidden behind the bamboo grove. Like so many times before, Mother and I had dropped by your house as we were passing by. We had been neighbours for as long as I could remember. But for the most part, we never spoke; rather, you never spoke to me. You were one of the older boys and perhaps I seemed just a child to you. But sometimes I would spot you with pretty Naro, who was no older than me. Mother would repeatedly warn me against getting too familiar with Naro and her friends who, she felt, were too precocious. She need not have bothered. I don't think Naro even knew my name. Para Medical colony, where we grew up, had an open rest stop beside the row of paan shops where youngsters would gather in the evenings and 'loiter', as Mother delicately puts it. I had a strict curfew and was never allowed to go there. But sometimes, while returning home late at night with Mother behind the wheel, I would enviously watch the place grow bright and alive, teeming with people, as the sun grew hazy and blue with sleep. I only began wanting to go there after that brief summer day. I wanted you to see me in your world.

My father passed a long time ago when I was only three and a half. 'Too young to remember!' I heard Mother remark once. But I do remember. I have memories of dark nights when my father carried me, tied with a cloth, against his strong back and his heavy shawl thrown over us, feeling warm and drowsy against him. In this memory, the skies were vast and always filled with enormous stars. I also remember his deep sonorous voice, singing, humming me to sleep. Once, while helping Mother rummage for old clothes to give away to a charity sale, I discovered an old Angami Lohe shawl and remembered those cold comforting nights. I didn't need a confirmation from Mother to know it was the shawl my father used to carry me to sleep, when he was alive.

My mother and yours were friendly with each other.

Although we regularly exchanged gifts during Christmas and shared food with other neighbours, I knew my mother liked yours especially because your Christmas cakes were always bigger and the prettiest casserole dish was always used to deliver your food. Your mother was such a gorgeous, elegant woman and mine once remarked that you had taken after her. Your father was much older and looked even older than his advancing years. But that might be because he had been sick for a long time. Our mothers grew especially close just months before our summer, after your father passed away. You looked so brave and handsome in your black suit during the funeral. You spoke briefly about your father's life and said that you were glad he was finally free of pain and at peace. The only time you gave yourself away was when your voice trembled towards the end, as you said your final goodbye.

The first time we spoke was when you and your mother visited us, a little more than a month after your father had passed. Your mother brought a lovely fruit basket to say thank you to mine for her kindness during the past weeks. While they spoke, I showed you my book collection and your eyes lit up when you spotted a bunch of DC and Marvel comic books underneath *A Tree Grows in Brooklyn* and a much-thumbed copy of Dahl's *Matilda*. You didn't think girls read super hero comic books too. You seemed satisfied with my explanation that we girls needed heroes just as much. I was thrilled to find something in common with you. I think our friendship began over comic books. From then on, we would exchange comics regularly and I began buying more DC and Marvel and less Mandy and Archie. It wasn't because I was in love with you. Not then. You were simply someone I looked up to and therefore, wanted to please.

But it all changed after that brief summer day outside your house. I dreamt about you for the first time that night. For the first time too, I didn't call you on the telephone the following day although I wanted to see you, to hear your voice. I waited for you. But you still hadn't called by dusk so I kept my new found pride aside and rang you. When you answered, I could hear laughter in the background. Clearly, your friends were over. I suddenly had a mental image of Naro holding a glass of something sweet, sickeningly pretty and coy beside you. So I found myself abruptly asking when you were returning my books as it had been more than a month since you borrowed them. I must have sounded brusque but instead of getting annoyed, you were apologetic and it made me feel petty. I made up an excuse about a friend at school wanting to borrow one of the books. I felt immensely lonely that night.

You came to see me a few days later. I wished you had called to check first; I would have liked to clean up a bit. I realized that's the problem with being neighbours. It's not that big a deal if the person is not home. You forgot to bring my books and I didn't ask. You seemed sullen but I didn't mind. You had come to see me! You didn't want to come inside and instead, asked whether I wanted to go for a walk. I quickly threw on a jacket and followed you out of the house. Down the main road, we took the lower, less trodden road that soon became kaccha footpath. You didn't speak much on the way, walking with determined strides, as if we actually had a destination. I was happy to follow, swinging a little stick, swatting at bushes and tree branches along the way. All of last night's heartsick loneliness was forgotten. Soon, we passed the woods and reached the edge of a cliff where, down below, was the National Highway 39 which led to Dimapur. Only then did you stop and sit down, cross legged, your elbows resting on your knees. I took my cue to sit beside you. I was panting heavily from our walk-turned-trek and when you noticed my breathlessness, you admonished:

'You should have asked me to slow down.'

I dismissed your apology with a shake of my head.

Restless, you got up, picked a few pebbles and threw them one by one, down onto the road below, aiming for a passing army truck and missing it.

'How did your father die?'

I was taken aback. You had never asked me about my father, not even when you saw his photograph at my house.

'Mother said he had been sick for a long time,' I answered, then added, 'Like yours, I guess.'

'Do you remember him?'

'Not really, I was really small when he died,' I mumbled.

Your back towards me, you turned and nodded, then gingerly picked another stone and threw it with feeling, this time hitting the trunk of a Rüpruó tree, right in the middle. At the same time, you blurted in a dull monotone voice, 'My mother's seeing someone.'

'Who?' I asked. I didn't know what else to say.

'Does it matter? My father's just recently died and it seems my dearest devoted mother just can't adjust to sleeping alone.' You were obviously upset now and the back of your fair neck grew dark red, giving away your rising emotions. When I didn't respond immediately, you began swearing loudly and said such nasty things about your mother that I felt shocked. I had never seen this side of you and felt a little scared.

'Don't talk about your mother like that! Imagine how hurt she'd be if she knew what you were saying.'

'You're supposed to be on my side! Why are you defending her? Anyway, forget it! I should have known you wouldn't understand. Your father's been gone far too long for you to comprehend how revolting it is to see your own mother debasing your father's memory!' You shouted the words and it made tears spring to my eyes. I was furious to hear you speak about my father so carelessly, as if his death mattered less as compared to yours because it had been long ago. I spluttered, unable to justify my anger but still livid. You looked incredulous when you saw my eyes brim with tears and only stopped short of calling me a baby. It made me feel even worse and I shouted at you and stormed off.

You didn't follow immediately but somehow caught up with me somewhere in between, in the middle of the woods. I had calmed down by then and so had you. Again, we walked in silence, this time, you trailing behind me. After a while, just as we were passing a stream, I felt cold water spray my back and heard laughter as I turned around in initial outrage. Soon, we were splashing about the shallow waters and you couldn't stop teasing me about being a crybaby earlier. Then later, resting atop a massive boulder by the edge of the stream, you took out a packet of Wills Classic and seemed pleased that the cigarette sticks inside were still dry even though the packet was soaking wet. You had a lighter wedged inside the half empty cigarette box. It was the first time I saw you smoke. Your light brown hair darkened with water fell over your forehead in smooth straight lines and I remember finding you so devastatingly attractive and grown up as you expertly twirled your lit cigarette between unusually slender fingers.

'Is Naro your girlfriend?' I asked, trying to sound casual

'Nah, she's just a friend,' you replied without looking at me, lightly flicking ash off the glowing tip of your cigarette.

Looking at me, you grinned mischievously and teased. 'I have you, don't I?' You made a face as you said it and not knowing how to flirt back, I blushed and looked away. I wished I could have said something clever and make sparkling conversation in return. I bet Naro would have known exactly what to say.

All the feelings from yesterday came rushing back. I went home that day, drenched and lighthearted. I couldn't stop myself from grinning foolishly, not even while Mother scolded me for coming home in such a state.

I was evasive when Mother asked what exactly you and I did that day and why we took so long. She appeared suspicious and for the first time, I hated her suffocating need to know my every passing thought and longed for some space in my life. I replayed our day in my head again and again, especially lingering over the nice things you said. I don't remember giving much thought over what you said about your mother.

You disappeared for days after that. I called but your mother said you were out. She wasn't her usual friendly self, sweetly apologetic, explaining how you were at your best friend Abeilie's place or playing games at Temjen's video arcade, or inviting me to visit like she always does whenever I ring. Instead, she sounded agitated and anxious to hang up. You didn't return my call and I agonized whether your mother had forgotten to inform you.

On my way back home from tuition one day, I bumped into your mother.

'Menguü, how lovely to see you! Are you coming back from tuitions?' she asked in her melodic voice.

I nodded and smiled.

'How is your mother? I've been meaning to visit her but have been so tied up lately.'

I suddenly remembered what you had told me and wondered whether it had anything to do with the new someone in her life but didn't ask. I did enquire about you though and your mother's light eyes clouded. She said you were fine but her voice faltered. Then she brightened up almost immediately and reached out to touch my shoulder with her long tapered fingers.

'Come over one of these days okay? We'll talk and gossip, just us girls!' she promised with a conspiratorial wink.

Somehow, I couldn't imagine my mother saying something like that without sounding ridiculous. On the way home, I suppressed laughter, hiding my face behind my Algebra textbook, at the cruel but involuntary image of my poor mother winking and acting all coy and girlish.

Mother seemed unusually thoughtful over dinner that night. Finally, she asked, just as I was finishing my last mouthful of rice and potato curry,

'Menguü, have you seen Jazo after that day at the river?'

I had told Mother that we'd gone to search for fish but had fallen in instead.

Mother explained that Aunty Grace and old Atsa Neidoü had visited her sometime during the afternoon. Over several cups of tea, the women had given her the latest neighborhood gossip. They lamented over how Uncle Tokato, a mean drunk, came home late last night and picked a fight with his wife. The pair created such a ruckus that the young Rengma couple next door alerted the others who finally intervened. 'How dare you all interfere?' Uncle Tokato had shouted 'She is my wife! I can do as I please with her.' But all this was nothing new. The latest gossip doing the rounds all over the neighbourhood, taking shape with each retelling, was how your mother was carrying on with Dr. Richard, the young doctor who had been caring for your father these past years. What was most scandalous was that people were saying that the affair had begun long before, while your father was still alive.

'Did Jazo mention anything to you?' Mother asked

I said no because then she would grill me as to why I didn't mention anything that day. Then Mother said that your next door neighbours, the Dasguptas, had seen you and the doctor getting into a scuffle almost a week back and that you had stormed out of your house as your mother stood in the doorway, looking both upset and mortified. The neighbours had not seen you come home since. That night, I thought about what you told me and wished I had handled it better when you first confided in me.

Knowing what I did now, I had to see you. I wanted to be there for you and this time, I would not fail. After tuitions the following day, I let loose my shoulder length hair and put on the light green hair band I had previously stuffed in my bag, which mother said brought out the brown in my eyes. I went to search for you at the rest spot where I knew you'd be. It took me a bit longer than expected and by the time I reached, it was already dark and there was a bonfire with flecks of orange flying up in the air, lighting up indistinct faces and figures around it. I suddenly felt self conscious. My single minded determination to find you had made me

recklessly bold. I turned to leave but then I saw you. You had
Naro on your lap with her arms around your neck. You were
all singing along to the energetic strumming of the guitar by
someone in your midst. Perhaps you felt my stare. I saw your
eyes widen and mouth slacken in surprise mid-song as you
spotted me. The others had not noticed and continued being
boisterous and gay. I wonder whether you saw the hurt in
my face. But how could you recognize something you were
completely oblivious to? Nevertheless, I was angry with you.
I was a child; an innocent, as you yourself had accused and
teased in turn. How could you be so charming with me and
expect me to remain unmoved?

I ran home in tears, so aware that you did not follow this
time or catch up either. Mother's wrath over my coming home
past curfew turned into concern when she saw my blotchy
tear-stained face. With my head on her lap, I confessed
everything; the anguish of first love and how badly you had
treated me, being my friend only when you needed me to be.
I was so angry I told Mother the awful things you had said
about your mother. Things I would never say about mine
and also about what you had said about my father being long
gone. Mother said nothing, consoling me, letting me pour
out all my childish rage and finally, when I was spent, she
held me as I drifted to sleep.

I woke with an ominous feeling of dread the following
morning. Mother was bustling about in the kitchen, already
dressed for work but still in her bedroom slippers. While
dropping me off to school, she told me that she had been
mistaken about you and your mother. And that I was not to
see you again. I nodded dumbly. What could I expect after

the things I had said last night? The way I had cried and raged about you.

You came to see me twice but Mother told you I was busy with homework. The second time you came, I peeped through our chiffon white curtains as you continued to linger after Mother had already closed the door. As if sensing my presence, you turned suddenly and our eyes met. But neither of us had anything to say and I backed away.

Your mother married Dr. Richard shortly after, amidst much scandalous gossip. She went to live with him at his house in another locality. We never saw her again. You kept refusing to move until finally, your paternal grandparents came to take you. But I didn't know all this until it was too late. The day you left, I came home from school to find a brown package on my study table. Inside were four DC comics and Verne's *Journey to the Centre of the Earth,* which I had purchased for your reading pleasure. I wish I had been there when you came to return my books. I wanted you to keep them. I would have liked you to take something that once belonged to me with you to your new life. And perhaps it would have healed something that was broken.

But you left, taking nothing and leaving too much behind.

I came across Naro not long after your abrupt departure. Her smile seemed sad. Or maybe it was simply a reflection of my own sadness. I took a deep breath and glanced upwards as the first leaves of autumn made their slow sorrowful descent towards the cold concrete pavement. Summer had come to an end.